# ROARING VALLEY

On his way home from New Mexico, Dan McCoy, Sheriff of Red Springs, comes to the rescue of Pat Goddard, only to find he has interfered in a domestic affair. Later, when she tries to get a message to him, Dan's curiosity is aroused and he finds himself helping to solve the murder of the owner of Roaring Valley. Russ Stanton, boss of the neighbouring Broken C, wants to gain full control of the whole range and Roaring Valley plays a key part in his plans. Double crossing, rustling and murder are all part of the malicious schemes Dan uncovers.

# ROARING VALLEY

# ROARING VALLEY

*by*

Jim Bowden

**Dales Large Print Books**
Long Preston, North Yorkshire,
BD23 4ND, England.

British Library Cataloguing in Publication Data.

Bowden, Jim
    Roaring Valley.

    A catalogue record of this book is
    available from the British Library

    ISBN    978-1-84262-643-6 pbk


First published in Great Britain in 1962 by Robert Hale Limited

Copyright © Jim Bowden 1962

Cover illustration © Gordon Crabb

The moral right of the author has been asserted

Published in Large Print 2009 by arrangement with
Mr W. D. Spence

Dales Large Print is an imprint of Library Magna Books Ltd.

Printed and bound in Great Britain by
T.J. (International) Ltd., Cornwall, PL28 8RW

# Chapter One

Dan McCoy pulled his horse to a halt. The tall, lithe, weather-beaten man with a tin star pinned on the left-hand side of his brown shirt rubbed the sweat from his face with his large handkerchief. He glanced skywards and was thankful that the sun was lowering towards the west and was already ceasing to beat the Texas countryside with intense ferocity.

As he eased himself in the saddle he glanced along the valley behind him. Suddenly he stiffened. About a mile away a cloud of dust billowed skywards. Dan pushed his horse forward to a group of huge rocks which stood close to the trail. He turned his horse out of sight behind them and drawing his spyglass from its leather holder he slipped from the saddle and scrambled quickly up the rocks. Reaching the top, he flattened himself and levelled his spyglass at the rapidly approaching cloud of dust. He took in the scene at a glance. Three cowboys pounded the trail in desperate pursuit of a lone rider and quirted their horses for more speed to close the hundred yards which separated them from the rider in front.

Dan turned his attention to the lone rider and he gasped with surprise when his spyglass revealed that the rider was a girl. Her slim figure was bent low over her horse's neck almost as if she was part of the animal. Unhesitatingly she kept the horse at full gallop anxious to maintain, if not increase, the distance between herself and her pursuers, but Dan realised that the three men were gaining steadily on her.

He scrambled down from his vantage point and was soon in the saddle holding his horse in check behind the rocks. The thunder of pounding hoofs grew louder and louder as the pursuit rapidly approached Dan's cover. As they flashed past him, two cowboys were already drawing alongside the girl, closing in on either side, whilst the third rider urged his horse ahead to cut across her path. The two men crowded the girl to a halt and, as horseflesh crashed against horseflesh, a terrified look crossed the girl's face. The cowboy on the right leaned forward and grabbed the reins from the girl's hand. She struck at him, but he ignored the blows as he held on to the leather until his companion leaned over and pinioned her arms to her side. She twisted and struggled, but she could not escape the hard, muscular grip.

McCoy slipped his Colt from its holster and pushed his horse forward on to the trail. The three men were so intent on controlling the girl and their sweating, restless horses, that they did not notice Dan until he was close to them. They looked round sharply, startled when they saw Dan, his gun menacing them, pull his horse to a halt.

'Jest leave go of the young lady,' snapped Dan.

Dark anger crossed the faces of the three cowboys. One of them moved his hand towards his holster, but as Dan's warning shot passed close to his hand, it froze to the butt.

'Don't try thet again,' snarled Dan. He glared at the cowboy who still held the girl. 'I'm waitin',' he said coldly.

Slowly, the man relaxed his grip and the girl pulled her horse round and rode alongside Dan.

'Thanks,' she said, her voice soft and clear.

A short hard-faced cowboy in a blue shirt leaned forward in his saddle. He glared angrily at Dan.

'Keep out of this, stranger,' he warned harshly. 'It's none of your business.'

'When I see a defenceless girl pursued by three cowpokes I make it my business,' answered Dan testily.

'Better fer you if you didn't,' came the reply. 'You could bring yourself a heap of trouble. You aren't from around these parts or you'd know not to meddle in Bill Goddard's affairs. An' thet tin star won't help you,' he nodded.

Dan ignored the remarks and spoke to the girl. 'Where you headin' for, Miss?' he asked.

'Silverton,' she replied as she adjusted her grey, flat-crowned sombrero on her short-cut auburn hair.

'Then I think you'd better get started whilst I keep these hombres here,' advised Dan.

'Hold it!' A commanding voice rasped behind them.

Grins spread across the faces of the three men in front of them and Dan glanced at the girl to see fright and disappointment in her deep blue eyes as she turned in the saddle.

'Drop thet gun!'

Dan obeyed the order without hesitation.

10

He realised from the tone of the voice that the newcomer would stand no nonsense. He eased himself in the saddle to see two men astride their horses a few yards away. A tall, broad-shouldered cowboy held a rifle levelled in Dan's direction. He saw that the other rider was a man in his early fifties, smartly dressed in working clothes. A checked shirt was partially covered by a fawn coloured vest which topped trousers of a matching colour neatly folded in the top of short riding boots. His Stetson, the wide brim of which was curled, was set neatly on his head. He pulled his horse to a halt in front of Dan but turned his attention to the girl.

'You were told not to leave the ranch, Pat,' he said firmly. Annoyance crept into his voice as he continued.

'I've enough work for my men to do without havin' them chase after you. Expect you were headin' for Silverton and Lance Peters!'

'Dad, I love him,' snapped the girl, 'and nothing you say or do will make me change my mind. You can't keep me on the ranch for ever.' Her eyes were wide and fired with anger.

'We'll talk about it at home,' her father

replied quietly. He turned to the three cow-boys. 'See that Pat gets home safely,' he ordered.

'Very well, Mister Goddard,' answered the ranch-hands.

They pushed their horses forward along-side the girl who looked round desperately for some means of escape. Her gaze met Dan's, a pleading look in her eyes but he knew it would be useless to attempt anything.

The rancher watched his daughter ride away before turning to Dan. He smiled. 'Guess you didn't know what you were ridin' into, son,' he said amiably. 'I'm Bill Goddard this here is my foreman, Dave Walters.'

Dan nodded to the two men and intro-duced himself. He saw Goddard glance at the tin star pinned to his shirt. 'From Red Springs,' he added.

'Way off your beat,' observed Goddard curiously.

'Had some business up in New Mexico; I'm on my way home,' explained Dan. 'I'm sorry if I cut in on a domestic affair, but three men ridin' down a girl, wal–'

Goddard laughed. 'Guess I'd hev done the same, son. I admire you for it. Truth is my daughter's a bit wild an' bent on marryin' someone who's not good enough for her.

This isn't the first time I've had to stop her runnin' off.'

'She sure gave your men a run fer their money,' laughed Dan.

Goddard smiled. 'Wal, I guess I'd better get back,' he said. 'So long, son, watch how you ride.'

Dan nodded his farewell to the two men who pulled their horses round and put them into a canter. He watched them for a few moments before swinging out of the saddle to retrieve his Colt. His face was thoughtful as he climbed into the saddle and sent his horse forward towards Silverton. A girl's face haunted him.

## Chapter Two

The evening sun was casting long shadows when Dan McCoy rode into Silverton. The horse's hoofs hardly stirred the dust as he rode slowly along the main street. He halted in front of the livery stable, slid from the saddle and led his horse inside. Once he was satisfied that the animal was comfortable for the night he made his way to the hotel where he paid in advance for a room for the night and ordered a hot bath.

Refreshed by the water and change of clothes, Dan left the hotel and strolled along the sidewalk enjoying the sharpness of the evening air as darkness closed over the Texas countryside. A light was burning in the sheriff's office and after knocking on the door Dan stepped inside to find the sheriff seated behind a desk examining some papers.

He was a man about thirty-five with a rugged but friendly face. His hair was greying at the temples, adding a distinguished look to the frank brown eyes which were sharp and alert. Dan saw his surprise as the

14

keen glance swept over him and rested on the star on Dan's chest. The young sheriff quickly introduced himself.

'Glad to know you, Dan.' The deep voice was full of sincerity. 'Matt Roberts. I was about to go, join me fer a drink?'

'Thanks,' replied Dan, 'but I'm ready for a good meal, been in the saddle all day. I'm on my way home to Red Springs from the Pecos country. I was on my way to the cafe when I saw your light.'

'All right, I'll come with you,' said Matt, 'an' then we'll go to the Golden Cage.' He turned down the lamp and blew out the light. After locking the office door, Matt Roberts led Dan to 'Anne's Cafe'.

'You'll get a good meal here,' said Matt as they reached the door. 'Nothing fancy, mind you, but you'll know you've hed somethin' to eat.'

The two men seated themselves at a table and Matt introduced Dan to Anne Denston an attractive woman of about Matt's age. She was neatly dressed in a checked gingham frock with a small white apron tied neatly round her waist. Her dark hair was showing signs of greying; her deep brown eyes set in an oval face sparkled, but Dan thought he detected a sadness deep down as if trouble had not passed Anne by untouched. After taking their order, Matt watched Anne go through the door to the kitchen before he spoke.

'Nice girl,' he said quietly. 'She's had it rough but life seems to be treating her a little more kindly now.'

'Guessed as much,' said Dan.

'Her husband had a small spread in Roaring Valley about ten miles from here,' explained Matt. 'Small but good and mighty important.'

'Important?' Dan raised his eyebrows as he put the query.

'Yes,' answered Matt. 'You see the Denstons owned all the valley and it separated the two big spreads, the Broken C and the Flying F. The valley had a marvellous water supply, both parties cast envious eyes on it.'

'Reckon there was the makings of trouble there,' commented Dan grimly.

'There sure was,' agreed the sheriff. 'Poor John Denston wanted to let both parties use the water at a price.'

'Reasonable?' asked Dan.

Matt nodded.

'Then why the trouble?' pressed Dan.

'Both spreads are bossed by stubborn men who want to be the sole cattle-king around here and each figured if he owned that water supply then he'd hold the upper hand.'

'And the Denstons were in the middle of it all,' mused Dan.

'Yeah. John had a rough time of it when he refused to sell out; cattle rustled, men beaten up, buildings destroyed – they tried the lot.'

'Couldn't you do anythin' about it?' asked Dan.

'We couldn't pin anythin' on either party,' replied Matt. 'And then John was killed.'

'How did thet happen?' asked Dan.

'No one knows. Poor Ann found him two miles from the house up the valley and–' Matt shut up as Anne approached with their meal. As he cut into a tender steak Matt continued.

'Of course, that was the end for Anne; she left the ranch an' set up this place on borrowed money.'

'Borrowed money?' Dan showed surprise at Matt's statement. 'But surely Anne got a tidy sum from one of the outfits?'

Matt's face was grim as he looked at Dan. 'Thet was the strange thing about it. When Anne got back after finding John's body, she found the house had been entered and the deeds to the ranch were missing. I figure that John was killed for those deeds.'

'Who got the valley?' asked Dan. 'Flying F or Broken C?'

'Neither,' replied Matt.

'What?' Dan stared incredulously at the sheriff.

'Fellow by the name of Clem McLane stepped in and snapped it up,' explained Matt. 'Been in town about three weeks; said he was lookin' fer a place to settle down.'

'But didn't the two big boys do anythin' about it?' asked Dan puzzled by the story.

'Little they could do. Flying F had just acquired another big section to the west and stocking it with cattle had drained their resources. Russ Stanton of the Broken C said he was in a similar predicament as regards buying – he was on a large overdraft from the bank.'

'This killin' seemed to happen at an opportune time,' commented Dan.

Matt nodded. 'I know what you're thinkin',' he said, 'but there was nothing to connect McLane with the crime.'

'Did the other two take this lying down?' asked Dan.

'There was a bit of trouble for a while but this died down,' explained Matt. 'Then, quite conveniently, McLane leased the water rights in the valley to Stanton! This virtually doubles the value of the west side of the Broken C and renders useless the east side of the Flying F.'

'This could have been a put up job between McLane and Stanton,' pointed out Dan.

'I thought of that,' agreed Matt, 'but there was no proof. Stanton pays McLane. I've been able to check that. Of course,' he added, 'McLane could repay Stanton.'

'Where did the Flying F fit into this?' asked Dan curiously.

'All appears fair and square, so there's nothing Bill Goddard can do about it,' explained the sheriff. Dan looked up curiously at the mention of Goddard. 'Bill is tough, will ride hard, and fight hard, if necessary, but he'll play it the right side of the law.' The lawman paused thoughtfully before he added. 'What he'd do if ever there was proof that Stanton an' McLane hed worked this together I don't know.'

'I summed Goddard up as tough when I met him back along the trail,' said Dan.

Matt looked sharply at Dan. 'How did you run across him?' he asked.

Dan related the story of his meeting with the rancher and the sheriff listened carefully as he enjoyed his meal. When Dan finished,

Matt shook his head slowly.

'It's a great pity,' he said. 'Bill rules that girl too firmly and she's a determined, stubborn youngster, gets it from her father I guess.' He paused as he drank some coffee. 'She's missed a mother around the ranch,' he continued. 'She died when Pat was born and Bill's had to bring her up. He'd set his heart on a boy so's there'd be someone to follow him, and he's tried to bring Pat up to take over the ranch. She's been raised amongst men, Dan, and Bill can't figure it out when she's kicked against it.'

'Who's this Lance Peters?' asked Dan.

'Rides for Wells Fargo,' explained Matt. 'A fine upright young chap; he and Pat seem sweet on each other, but there again Bill doesn't see Lance Peters as a cattleman. He has ideas for Pat to marry Stanton.'

'Stanton?' Dan gasped in amazement. 'But I thought they were at each other.'

'Wal, not exactly against each other. As far as I know they fight it square, as I said Bill walks the right side of the law. Stanton, I'm not so sure about, but I can't prove anything. The situation's explosive particularly if Stanton and McLane are working together.' Matt drained his coffee and laughed. 'I'm sorry for boring you with our troubles,' he

20

said. 'Let's go and have a drink over at the Golden Cage.'

Dan smiled. 'You've certainly not bored me. I was most interested, particularly after meeting Pat and her father. I nearly put my foot in a domestic quarrel.'

'Just as well you didn't go any further,' observed the Sheriff. 'Goddard can be pretty rough if anyone kicks against him.'

The two men rose from the table and gathered their Stetsons from the hooks on the wall. They walked over to the counter and paid Anne for the meal.

'I'll call for you in an hour, Anne,' said Matt.

Anne smiled and nodded. 'Thanks, Matt.'

As they left the cafe Matt explained. 'I generally see Anne home,' he said. 'She has a little house on the edge of town and I don't like her going in on her own in the dark.'

'Seems a nice person,' commented Dan. 'A pity those deeds couldn't be found.'

The two men spent a pleasant hour yarning as they enjoyed a drink in the saloon. When Matt called for Anne, Dan bade them both goodnight and strolled casually along the sidewalk in the direction of the hotel.

As he crossed the end of a dark alley, a

block from the hotel, a hand touched him on the arm. Startled, Dan swung round, his hand moving swiftly towards his holster. He had scarcely touched the butt when an elderly, bearded cowboy stepped from the blackness of the alley.

'Hold it!' rasped a hoarse voice quietly. At the same time a boney hand gripped Dan's as he touched his Colt. Dan relaxed, and eased his grip when he saw the old man more clearly.

'What is it?' asked Dan puzzled by the intrusion, and more surprised by the way the man glanced anxiously around before speaking.

There was a half-frightened look in his eyes as he stared at Dan. 'Pat Goddard wants you to contact...'

The words were lost as the quietness of the night was shattered by the roar of a Colt from the blackness of the alley. The old man staggered, clasped his side, a surprised look crossed his face as his eyes widened. His lips continued to move forming words but uttering no sound. He slumped forward against Dan and would have slid to the ground had not the young man's powerful arms supported him.

Quickly, the young sheriff dragged the

stranger away from the alley entrance to the shelter of the neighbouring building but as he laid him down, Dan knew the man was dead.

## Chapter Three

The sound of running footsteps pounded louder and louder in Dan's ears as he bent over the still form. He was only dully aware of the man who had stopped beside him.

'What happened?' snapped a voice startling Dan back into reality.

He glanced upwards over his shoulder to see Matt Roberts towering over him. Dan stood up quickly.

'This fellow stopped me at the corner; told me that Pat Goddard wanted me to contact someone, but he was shot before he told me who,' explained Dan. 'Know him?'

Matt nodded his face grim as he stared at the still form in the dust.

'Cal Smithson,' he whispered. Any further explanation was halted as Anne Denston hurried up to the two men. She gasped when she saw the old man and gripped Matt's arm tightly.

'Shot in the back,' she whispered hoarsely. 'Just like John.'

Matt turned her quickly but gently away

from the body. He ordered two of the cowboys who had hurried to the scene to take care of the dead man and he quickly made a mental note of the men who had gathered together.

'Dan,' said Matt turning to the young sheriff from Red Springs. 'I'd like a word with you.'

Dan nodded and joined Anne and Matt as they walked away from the grim scene. They hurried along the boards in silence and it wasn't until they reached the gate of the house that Anne spoke.

'You'd better both come in,' she said quickly. 'A cup of coffee would do us all good.'

'Thanks,' said Matt pushing open the gate.

The two men followed Anne into the house where she reached for some matches on a table just inside the door. She scraped a match on the box and as it spluttered and flared Dan saw that Anne's face was white. The light dimmed momentarily as the girl applied it to the wick but brightened as she turned it up. Anne led the way into the kitchen and soon had some coffee ready for them.

'Can't understand anyone wanting to kill

poor old Cal Smithson,' puzzled Matt. His brow puckered and he looked thoughtfully at Dan. 'Could it have been meant fer you?' he asked.

Dan showed surprise at the suggestion. 'Me? I can't see why anyone around here should want to kill me. It's the first time I've been this way.'

'Anything happen back on the trail that you haven't told me about?' asked Matt.

The young man looked thoughtful for a few moments then slowly shook his head. 'Nothing thet warranted me being shot at.'

'You didn't cross any of Goddard's men?' quizzed Matt.

'No,' replied Dan. 'Why should Goddard's riders want to kill me?'

'That I don't know,' answered Matt rubbing his chin thoughtfully. 'But old Cal has been at the Flying F ever since Goddard moved out here. I was wondering if he had to attract your attention whilst someone else put a slug in you.'

'Whoever it was was a mighty poor shot in thet case,' laughed Dan. 'I think you're on the wrong horse, Matt. Someone wanted to stop Cal giving me thet message.'

'But who?' puzzled Matt. 'It doesn't figure that Goddard's men would shoot one of their own and yet who else could have known he was bringing a message to you?'

'There's only one way to find out,' said Dan emphatically, 'an' thet's to call on Pat Goddard.'

'Thet will hev to wait until morning,' replied Matt.

'Not likely,' rapped Dan. 'I figure we want to see her on her own, if we wait until morning we might not get thet chance; we've got to sneak in tonight.'

The two men pushed themselves away from the table and as Matt picked up his Stetson, Anne placed her hand on his.

'Be careful, Matt,' she whispered, her eyes reflecting her unspoken thoughts that what had happened to Cal Smithson may happen to him.

Matt smiled. 'I'll be all right,' he said reassuringly.

The two men crossed to the door but before opening it Matt halted Dan. He looked searchingly at the sheriff from Red Springs.

'McCoy,' he said firmly, 'this is really no concern of yours an' you'll want to be on your way tomorrow so I won't hold anything against you if you leave this to me.'

Dan smiled. 'I appreciate your thought,

27

Matt,' he replied, 'but when someone's shot whilst talkin' to me I like to know why an' I'd like to know what thet message was an' why Pat Goddard should pick on me.' He turned and looked at Anne. 'Besides, I reckon Anne would feel better if I went along with you.'

Anne smiled at the two men. Matt grinned at Dan and slapped him on the arm.

'All right,' he said. 'Glad to hev you along.'

The two men swung out of the door and hurried along the sidewalk to the livery stables where they soon had their horses saddled. They left Silverton at a brisk trot along the trail by which Dan had entered the town and they soon passed the place where Dan had met Goddard. The trail forked a mile further along and Matt led Dan along the left hand fork which took them further into the valley. The trail twisted through several low spurs of hills which sloped from the hillside bordering the valley on their right. A thin veil of cloud covered the moon and when Matt slowed his horse to a halt half a mile beyond the hills, Dan saw they were on the edge of a long slope which fell gently to the floor of the valley.

He could make out the black mass of buildings and beyond them a silvery reflection indicated the waters of Tule River. 'The Flying F,' whispered Matt. 'A beautiful place; a wonderful ranch. No wonder Goddard doesn't want to see it slip out of his family.' Dan detected a tone of regret in Matt's voice.

'Anything wrong?' he asked.

The sheriff gave a low laugh. 'No,' he replied. 'Just thet I had a chance of a ranch up in Wyoming; wish I'd taken it, but Texas held me.'

'Maybe you'll end up in Roaring Valley when this is cleared up,' chaffed Dan.

Matt grinned. 'Maybe,' he mused, and pushed his horse forward down the slope. The lawmen rode at a steady pace until they reached a line of cottonwoods about half a mile from the buildings.

'Reckon we'd better leave the horses here,' whispered Matt, pulling his mount to a stop.

The two men slipped from the saddles, tied the animals to the branch of a tree, and walked stealthily forward towards the buildings. Dan tensed himself, his eyes probing the darkness ahead for any sign of movement. They paused when they reached the fence about two hundred yards from the buildings. A light shone from a long low building, and from the chatter which came through the open window, Dan judged it to be the bunkhouse. He turned his attention to a building which stood apart from the rest, but all was darkness on this side.

'Know which is Pat's room?' asked Dan, his voice scarcely audible. Matt shook his head.

Dan put his hands on the top rail of the fence, and was about to pull himself up, when Matt gripped his arm. A stream of light flooded from the bunkhouse as the door was flung open. The lawmen froze, scarcely daring to breathe. Two cowboys moved through the light, closed the door behind them, and walked towards a neighbouring building. As the two men passed out of sight Dan and Matt flattened themselves to the ground. A few anxious minutes passed before the two cowboys reappeared leading two horses. They climbed into the saddles and turned their mounts to ride towards the river.

The lawmen breathed more freely and eased themselves from the ground.

'Must be goin' to relieve two men ridin' watch on the herd,' said Matt, hitching up his belt. 'We must move fast before the others ride in.'

The two men swung over the fence and

bending double ran swiftly to the ranch-house. Once in the shadows, they flattened themselves against the wall. They paused a moment listening for any sound, but only the noise from the bunkhouse broke the stillness. Dan drew his Colt and nudged the sheriff to follow him. The two men crept cautiously to the corner of the house; Dan peered round carefully and seeing no one about, moved silently towards the front of the house. Reaching the corner the two men halted and paused briefly before Dan inched forward to look round the corner.

He saw that a veranda ran the full length of the building but the four chairs placed near the door were unoccupied. The window nearest the corner was open, and the dim light which shone from it indicated that the curtains were drawn.

Dan motioned to Matt to stay where he was, and slowly eased himself over the veranda rail, and crept quietly towards the window.

'...and so thet's the position, Dave.' Dan recognised Bill Goddard's voice as he addressed his foreman. 'I reckon we can start movin' cattle on to the east range.'

'But are you sure you can trust Stanton?' queried Dave Walters. The note of doubt in the foreman's voice was in marked contrast to the confident note of his boss.

'He can't refuse his father-in-law,' replied Goddard with a laugh. If he tries to – which he won't – then Pat would have somethin' to say about it.'

'I just ain't sure of Stanton,' answered Walters. 'I think he was in with Clem McLane and put him up to gettin' Roaring Valley.'

Goddard laughed loudly. 'Nonsense,' he retorted. 'McLane was a stranger around here; he was smart an' stepped in when neither Stanton nor I could buy an' then Stanton outsmarted me by persuadin' McLane to let him hev exclusive rights to the water.'

'I still think thet it was a put up job between 'em,' muttered the foreman.

'They wouldn't be around here long if I thought that,' replied Goddard fiercely. His tone changed to one of amusement. 'But now I've outsmarted Stanton – he can't refuse me when he marries my daughter.'

'Don't be too sure, Mr Goddard,' replied Walters. 'I only hope you're right. We'll start movin' the cattle as you say.'

Realising the conversation was coming to an end, Dan eased himself upwards from his crouching position. He carefully turned back the edge of the curtain and saw Goddard pouring out two drinks. He glanced quickly round the room, lowered the curtain and swiftly made his way back to Matt. He motioned him towards the back of the building.

'She's not in there,' he whispered, 'only Goddard and his foreman. Seems Goddard has it all fixed up for Pat to marry Stanton. C'm on let's see if we can locate her.'

The two men moved slowly along the back of the house, pausing at each window to listen, but it was not until they turned the other corner that they heard the sound of sobbing coming from an open window.

'Wait here,' whispered Dan, and eased himself over the low window-sill into the room.

In the faint light, he could make out the figure of a girl lying face downwards on a bed. Her face was buried in her arms, and pillows, and as Dan moved silently forward, he could see her body shaking as she cried. The young sheriff paused a moment when he reached the bed. He regretted having to frighten the girl, but he must be sure she did not scream and betray his presence.

Suddenly he dropped on to the bed beside her, pushing her head harder into the pillow, stifling the cry which sprang to her lips. Quickly, he whispered reassuringly in her ear.

'It's all right, Pat, I'm the lawman you met this afternoon. You sent me a message, I'm here to help.'

Dan relaxed his grip, and the girl turned her head to see the young man rising to his feet. Her eyes, wide with fright, stared incredulously at Dan. Slowly, her tensed body relaxed, and she pushed herself round to sit on the edge of the bed. She wiped the tears from her eyes, red with crying.

'I didn't expect to see you again,' she whispered. 'And why through the window?'

It was Dan's turn to be surprised. 'But the message?' he said.

'Didn't you tell Lance?' asked Pat.

'Lance?' Dan was puzzled. 'I never got all the message.' He paused when he saw the look of astonishment on Pat's face. 'Haven't you heard?' he continued. 'Cal was shot when he was talking to me.'

'What!' Pat gasped. She sprang to her feet, staring unbelievingly at Dan.

'Steady,' he said. 'Keep it quiet, your father doesn't know we're around, thet's why I used the window. I wanted a word with you without him knowing.'

'Poor old Cal,' murmured Pat, sinking back on to the bed. 'Who did it?' she asked, looking up at Dan.

'Don't know,' he replied. 'We thought you might be able to help us.'

'Me?' Pat looked puzzled. 'And who's we?' she added.

'I've Sheriff Roberts with me; he's keeping watch outside the window,' replied Dan, nodding in the direction of the window. 'I figured someone was stopping Cal delivering that message, and not knowin' what it was I guessed we'd better see you alone.'

'I told Cal to ask you to contact Lance Peters and tell him what happened this afternoon,' explained the girl. 'I thought he would know what to do.' A shiver ran through her body. She shrugged her shoulders. 'It doesn't matter now, and poor Cal has been killed for nothing.'

Dan stared at the girl. 'What do you mean?'

'I've agreed to marry Russ Stanton, boss of the Broken C,' whispered Pat, her voice low, as if she hated what she was saying. The words choked in her throat, she shuddered and straightening herself she continued. 'Stanton doesn't know yet, but he'll be pleased, and so is my father.'

'But out there on the trail this afternoon, I thought you said you were going to marry Lance Peters,' exclaimed Dan.

Pat nodded. 'I was,' she sighed, 'but now things have changed.'

Dan started to speak, but Pat silenced him.

'Go home,' she said. 'Things are settled here; it's not your business, so forget it.'

'But why should Cal be shot? Why hadn't I to receive your message? Why shouldn't Lance be told about what happened today?' The questions came fiercely from Dan's lips.

Pat rose from the bed and stood in front of Dan. She looked at him straight in the eyes.

'I don't know why Cal should be killed. Lance will hear soon enough that I am going to marry Stanton, so please forget everything.' Dan's protestations were stopped when Pat looked at him pleadingly. 'Please,' she whispered.

Dan shrugged his shoulders and crossed the room to the window. He was about to stride over the window-sill when the sound of a hard-ridden horse broke the quietness.

'Someone in a mighty hurry,' he whispered.

Pat was at his side listening carefully.

'Get Sheriff Roberts inside quickly,' she

urged. 'Whoever it is is approaching the house from this side.'

Dan called softly to Matt, who was soon in the room beside them. The beat of the hoofs grew louder, and Dan saw a rider pounding towards the house. A door banged, and Pat knew that the noise of the approaching horse had attracted her father's attention. She heard a door open, and the sound of feet on the veranda.

'Maybe you had better go out, too,' whispered Dan to Pat. 'If your father comes looking for you, we don't want him to find us here.'

The girl nodded, and as the rider passed out of their sight to pull his horse to a halt in front of the veranda, Pat hurried from the room.

'Brought news of Cal's death,' whispered Pat, when she reappeared a few minutes later. 'Dad's swearing vengeance on the killer, wanted to ride into town to see the sheriff, but I got him persuaded to wait until morning.'

'Good,' praised Dan. 'Are you sure there's nothin' we can do to help?' he added.

'Help is not needed now,' replied the girl quietly, but firmly.

Matt glanced sharply at Dan, who slapped

37

the sheriff on the arm. 'C'm on,' he said.

The two men climbed out of the window and hurried cautiously away from the buildings. They climbed the fence swiftly, and lengthened their stride towards the line of cottonwoods. As they neared the trees, Dan suddenly grabbed Matt's arm and dragged him to the ground.

'Still!' he commanded urgently, and pointed in the direction of the trees.

A shadowy form moved slowly amongst the cottonwoods towards the horses.

Dan nudged the Sheriff of Silverton, and the two men crept swiftly forward Indian fashion. Once they reached the line of trees the lawmen rose to their feet and using the trees as cover moved quickly after their quarry. From the way the man was acting, Dan knew that he had seen the horses.

'Mustn't let him get near them,' whispered Matt.

The cowboy in front halted and from a position between two trees, was watching the horses carefully. He settled himself more comfortably, and eased his Colt in its holster.

'Waitin' for us,' whispered Matt, as the lawmen watched him from the cover of some shrubs.

'He's in for a surprise,' grinned Dan, who

drew his Colt from its holster and eased himself forward.

Matt followed close behind, and watched the young sheriff glide silently forward to the tree immediately behind the unsuspecting cowboy. When Matt joined him Dan indicated to him to remain where he was. Matt nodded and drew his Colt. About twenty yards of open space lay between Dan and the cowboy, and Matt Roberts admired the way Dan quickly, but silently, covered the ground.

The man never knew what hit him as Dan crashed the barrel of his Colt across the man's head. He slumped forward against the trees, and slid to the ground.

As soon as he saw the man fall Matt ran to Dan.

'Shorty Best. One of Goddard's men,' he said quietly.

'I know, saw him on the trail this afternoon,' answered Dan recognising the short, dark, hard-faced man who had ridden Pat Goddard down earlier that day. 'C'm on,' he continued, 'let's ride. Hope he didn't recognise the horses.'

'Couldn't tell mine from a dozen others round here,' said Matt, 'but your black – well, that's another matter!'

## Chapter Four

The two men untied their horses quickly, swung into the saddles, and put the animals into a fast gallop towards Silverton. They rode without speaking, and eased the pace only when they reached the town.

As they pulled up outside Anne Denston's the door opened and a shaft of light stabbed the darkness. The lawmen saw Anne standing in the doorway, and they hurried up the path to meet her.

'You shouldn't have waited up,' said Matt as they entered the house.

'I couldn't have slept,' replied Anne, leading the way to the kitchen where a pot of coffee was keeping hot on the stove.

As the two men sat down at the table Matt looked hard at Dan. 'Wal, let's have it,' he said. 'Where does Pat Goddard fit into all this?'

'She told Cal to tell me to contact Lance Peters,' explained Dan. 'I was to tell him what happened this afternoon. She expected him to do something.'

'But why did she say she didn't want any help?' puzzled Matt.

'She's agreed to marry Stanton!' replied Dan.

'What!' Matt gasped. 'But I thought she said she'd marry Lance Peters.'

'So did I,' said Dan.

'Don't forget Stanton courted Pat for some time,' said Anne, pouring out some coffee.

'Yeah, I know,' answered Matt, 'and she turned him down,' he added emphatically.

'A girl's entitled to change her mind,' answered Anne.

'Maybe,' mused Matt, sipping his coffee, 'but it doesn't ring true. What do you say, Dan?'

'If Pat's made up her mind, then surely that's the end of the matter,' put in Anne before the young sheriff from Red Springs could answer. 'Dan may as well forget it, and ride home tomorrow as planned.'

'I don't think the matter is settled,' replied Dan quietly. 'I agree with you, Matt, there's something queer about the whole thing.' He paused for a moment, stirring his coffee thoughtfully before looking up at Anne. 'And I wouldn't be surprised to find you and Roaring Valley fit into this somewhere.'

Anne's eyes widened with surprise. 'Roaring Valley?' she exclaimed. 'But how?'

Dan shook his head. 'I don't know, but I figure thet there's more trouble comin' an' I'll hev my share.'

Seeing the girl looking puzzled, Matt told her of their encounter with Shorty Best. As Matt finished, Dan pushed himself up from his chair.

'Wal, I don't think Goddard will move until mornin' so I figure I'll get some sleep,' he said. He picked up his Stetson, and turned towards the door.

'I think you'd better stay here,' advised Matt. 'If Goddard comes…'

'He'll come lookin' fer me,' interrupted Dan. 'But I'm not that important that he'll come tonight,' he added with a grin. Dan opened the door, and turned to his friends. 'Goodnight to you both, I'll see you in the morning,' he said, and stepped out into the night.

Matt looked at the door as it closed behind the young man. He shook his head slowly. 'He doesn't know Goddard like I do,' he whispered half to himself.

As the faint clop of Dan's horse faded along the street, Matt suddenly turned to Anne. 'I'm goin' to take a room next to his,' he said firmly, and grabbing his Stetson, hurried from the house.

Shorty Best moved his hand slowly to his head. His brain pounded as if a huge hammer was beating on it. He raised his face from the ground and rolled slowly over. The effort was almost too much for him, and he lay on his back breathing deeply. Slowly his brain cleared, and his eyes focused on the trees around him. It was a few moments before he realised where he was.

He sat up quickly, and cursed loudly when he saw that the horses had gone. Shorty pushed himself from the ground, and with the aid of a tree pulled himself to his feet. His head swam with the effort, and he paused a few moments, summoning his strength. Slowly he picked up his Stetson and stumbled away from the cottonwoods in the direction of the ranch-house.

There was no one about as he staggered to the door on which he hammered with his fist, calling loudly for Mister Goddard.

Feet pounded in the house and when he flung open the door Bill Goddard stared in amazement at Shorty, who leaned against the door post.

'What the...' His exclamation was cut short

as the cowboy's knees buckled, pitching him into Goddard's powerful arms. 'Dave, give me a hand,' he called to his foreman who had followed him along the corridor.

As the two men carried the cowboy into the house, Pat appeared from her room.

'What's all the noise...?' The question froze on her lips when she saw the unconscious Shorty. She stared wide-eyed at her father. 'What's happened, Dad?' she asked.

'Don't know,' replied the rancher. 'Get some water, quick.'

The girl hurried to the kitchen and the two men carried the cowboy into the room and laid him on the sofa. Dave Walters dropped to his knee, and examined Shorty's head.

'He's had a nasty crack,' he said looking up at his boss who leaned over the sofa back, 'but he'll be all right.'

Pat was soon back with a bowl of water, and she bathed the wound carefully. Goddard forced some brandy between Shorty's lips when Walters returned. The liquid burned its way through his mouth and throat and drove life back into his brain. He coughed and spluttered and attempted to sit up, only to find firm hands forcing him back on to the sofa.

'Steady, Shorty, take it easy. You'll be all right.'

The reassuring words pierced his dazed mind. His eyes flickered open and, as they focused, he saw Goddard and Walters standing over him.

'Sorry I passed out, Mister Goddard,' he apologised in a whisper.

'It's all right, Shorty,' replied the rancher. 'Have another drink of this,' he said, holding out the glass of brandy.

Shorty sipped steadily and eased himself on the sofa.

As he passed the glass back to Goddard, the rancher smiled. 'Feel like tellin' us what happened?' he asked.

The man nodded. 'I was down by the cottonwoods when I spotted two horses,' he explained. 'There was no one with them, so thought I'd wait. I'd just got settled when – wal, thet's all I remember, until I came to.'

Goddard looked sharply at Walters and then back to Shorty. 'Didn't you see anyone?' he asked.

'No,' answered the cowboy. He paused, a thoughtful look on his face. 'But, there was somethin'.' He rubbed his stubbled chin as he tried to recall what had impressed him in the cottonwoods. Suddenly he snapped his fingers. 'I've got it, it was thet horse.'

'What about it?' asked Walters eagerly.

'I've seen it before,' answered Shorty, excitement in his eyes. 'A big powerful black.'

'Who has a black around here?' snapped Goddard.

'It's not from around here I'm sure,' replied Shorty, trying to force himself to remember.

'It must be, if you've seen it before,' said Pat Goddard, moving forward to her father's side.

Shorty stared at her. 'I've got it!' he cried. 'Miss Pat reminded me. Thet lawman on the trail this afternoon!'

'What!' Goddard gasped. 'It can't be. What would he be doin' here?'

'I'll swear it was, Mister Goddard,' said Shorty.

'Recognise the other horse?' asked Walters.

'Same as many round here,' answered the wounded man.

Goddard looked thoughtful. Suddenly he turned to his foreman. 'Dave, Slim said this lawman was with Cal when he was shot. Get three of the boys, we'll see if this hombre's still in town!'

Goddard kept the pace fast until he drew

rein a quarter of a mile from town. His face was grim as his riders pulled to a halt alongside him.

'We don't know if this lawman had anythin' to do with Cal's killin' but we'd better be ready fer anythin'. Ed an' Mal take the back of the hotel. Wes, cover the front. Dave, come with me.'

The men nodded grimly, and without a word stabbed their horses into a gentle trot to the town. Only the odd light gleamed from a window when they rode slowly up the main street. Swinging from the saddles in front of the hotel they hitched their horses to the rail and the three cowboys moved quickly to their appointed positions, whilst Bill Goddard and his foreman strolled into the hotel unaware that their arrival had been noticed from a first floor window.

The two men crossed the dimly lit lobby to the desk, behind which the clerk dozed in a chair. Dave Walters reached across the desk and shook the man by the shoulder. A startled splutter escaped from his lips as he jerked upright.

'Good evening, Mister Goddard,' he gasped apologetically, jumping to his feet. 'I'm sure...'

'Have you a lawman, stranger to these

parts, stayin' here?' interrupted the rancher.

The clerk stared at the questioner. 'Well, I, er … I…' he stuttered.

'Have you, or haven't you?' snapped Walters, leaning forward on the desk.

The bespectacled clerk recoiled from the menacing look of the Flying F foreman. 'Yes, yes,' he spluttered. 'Room 4.'

The two men spun on their heels, and hurried up the stairs. A light shone from under the door of room 4. Goddard and Walters drew their Colts, flung open the door, and stepped quickly into the room.

Dan McCoy, who was sitting up in bed reading the local paper, which he had borrowed from the hotel clerk, gasped as the door burst open, and automatically reached for his Colt, hanging in its holster from the bed head.

'Leave it!' snapped Goddard.

Dan froze at the warning, then slowly eased himself in the bed, his eyes narrowing as he stared at the intruders.

'What's the idea?' he hissed.

'Certain things hev happened around here since you rode into town,' answered Goddard, 'an' I'd like to ask you a few questions.'

'Git on with it then,' snapped Dan, 'but I

don't guarantee an answer.'

'Not here,' said Goddard coolly. 'At my ranch, so on your feet.'

A faint smile of contempt flicked across Dan's face. 'I aren't movin' from my bed,' he replied testily.

Dave Walters, his face darkening angrily, stepped forward, grasped Dan by the arm and dragged him from the bed. 'You'll do as Mister Goddard says, an' like it,' he snarled.

'He won't!' The quiet voice came from behind them.

Goddard and Walters spun round to see Sheriff Roberts, Colt in hand, standing in the doorway. Walters jerked his gun upwards, but before he could press the trigger it was sent spinning from his hand as Matt's Colt roared. Matt crouched, his eyes watching Goddard.

'Don't do it, Bill,' he snapped.

Slowly Goddard relaxed, and slipped his Colt back into its holster.

'Thanks, Matt,' said Dan, scrambling to his feet. 'How did you know?'

'Jest as well I booked a room next to you,' grinned the sheriff. 'Reckon my hunch was right.' He turned to Goddard. 'I guess I'll ease your mind,' he said.

The rancher, a puzzled look on his face,

stared at Roberts. 'What do you know about this hombre?' he snapped.

'Wal, Cal was shot by someone down the alley and as I've been with McCoy since then, I can vouch for all his movements.'

'But his horse was seen near my ranch, an' Shorty was gun whipped,' said Goddard.

'I know, I was with him,' announced Roberts easily.

'What!' Goddard gasped.

Dan glanced sharply at the sheriff, wondering how much of the truth he would tell Goddard.

'Dan offered his help,' continued Matt and the tension eased in Dan as the sheriff lied. 'We trailed the killer to your ranch, but lost his trail down by the cottonwoods, so we left the horses whilst we searched. Dan saw someone prowlin' around an' gun whipped him thinkin' it might be the killer who had doubled back on his tracks. Of course I recognised Shorty…'

'Why didn't you bring him in?' snapped Goddard.

'Wal, I'd found the trail an' we figured Shorty would be all right when he came to,' explained Matt.

Walters looked suspiciously at the sheriff. 'If you picked up his trail again, what are you doin' here?'

'It hadn't been easy to follow in the dark an' we lost it again half a mile further on. We figured we'd do better in daylight, so here we are,' replied Matt.

Goddard looked hard at the sheriff. 'Matt,' he said firmly. 'You and I have known each other a long time; I'll take your word but I reckon there's somethin' else you aren't tellin' me.' He paused, hoping for some explanation from Roberts, but when it was not forthcoming, he turned to his foreman. 'C'm on, Dave, we're at the wrong end of a Colt here.' He walked to the door, but before opening it he turned to the sheriff. 'I want Cal Smithson's killer,' he said grimly, 'and I don't want to hev to do your job fer you!'

## Chapter Five

The faint streaks of dawn were breaking the eastern horizon when Shorty Best rode swiftly from the Flying F, and headed in the direction of Roaring Valley. He had spent a fairly comfortable night, but his head still throbbed when he slipped quietly out of the bunkhouse before anyone else was awake. There was a purposeful urgency about his ride as he kept his mount to a brisk pace.

Five miles from the ranch-house the rolling range gave way to more broken country, through which Shorty threaded his way, before pulling his horse to a halt on the edge of a wide valley which narrowed and lifted towards the north. A ranch-house nestled under the spur of a hill to his left, and seeing much activity in its vicinity, Shorty pulled his horse round, and rode northwards, deciding that his crossing of Roaring Valley would be better unseen by Clem McLane or any of his riders. After riding for about three miles he turned his horse down the slope, and reaching the valley without mishap he put his horse into a gallop. Soon he was twisting his way up the opposite side of the valley to ride over the top of the ridge on to Broken C range.

Shorty urged his horse faster and the animal stretched itself across the ground in the direction of the Broken C ranch. Cowboys were preparing to leave for the range when Shorty galloped up to the long, low, ranch-house situated close to a swift flowing stream. As soon as the hard-faced cowboy pulled to a halt in front of the house he stepped from the saddle and strode on to the veranda. He rapped urgently on the door, and a few moments later it was opened by a dark-haired man of about thirty-five.

'Shorty!' he gasped. 'What...'

'It's urgent, Mister Stanton,' cut in Shorty.

'Come in,' said Stanton, and led the way into a big well-furnished room, where the touch of ease and luxury always made Shorty feel out of place.

Stanton picked up a box from the desk and offered Shorty a cheroot.

'Wal, Shorty, what brings you here?' he asked.

As the cowboy reported the events of the previous day he watched Stanton light his cheroot and could not help admiring him immaculately dressed in a dark blue silk shirt topping black jeans, which were neatly folded into the tops of black leather boots. A black, decorated butt protruded from a bright studded holster, and Shorty knew that men had been deceived by the fanciness.

'Why shoot Cal Smithson?' snapped Stanton, pacing up and down.

'I overheard Miss Pat tellin' him to contact this lawman, and tell him to inform Lance Peters what had happened on the trail,' explained Shorty. 'I thought it would be better if that message wasn't delivered.'

Stanton bit his lip. 'I guess you did,' he said. 'You needn't have worried, Peters is out of town, an' I guess this lawman wouldn't have stuck around. Now he might.'

'He sure is,' answered Shorty, feeling his head. He went on to tell Stanton of his encounter with Dan the previous evening.

Stanton rubbed his chin, and puffed thoughtfully at his cheroot.

'There's nothin' we can do about him, unless he makes a move,' he said. 'We'll carry on as planned. You git back to the Flying F, an' let me know as soon as Goddard moves any cattle.'

'Right, boss,' said Shorty, and picking up his battered, brown Stetson, he left the

Broken C.

Dan McCoy was awake early, and, as he ate his breakfast, he puzzled over the events which seemed to have been touched off by his meeting with Pat Goddard. It was not long before he decided to take a closer look at Roaring Valley, and the Broken C.

He rode at a steady pace across Goddard's land, but kept well away from the men of the Flying F who were tending the huge herds of cattle which grazed peacefully on the lush grassland. As he moved nearer Roaring Valley, the range became rougher, and the grass thinner, and it was somewhat of a surprise to Dan when he found himself on the edge of the range looking down into a wide lush green valley, through which flowed a fast-moving, sparkling river. The valley narrowed to his right, and Dan pulled his horse round, deciding to ride to the head of the valley. As he rode further north he realised more and more, what a wonderful place the Denstons had picked for their home, and what a marvellous site they had chosen to build their house, under the spur of a hill. Not wishing to be seen, Dan swung away from the edge of the hill as he passed the house, but turned back to the ridge about a mile further on. The ground became more and more broken, and, as he rode round a small hillock, he saw a rider drop over the hilltop at the other side of the valley.

Dan watched the man handle his horse skilfully down the steep slope, and put it into a steady gallop across the valley. Suddenly, he realised that the rider was heading in his direction, and that if he kept a straight course he would come over the hill close to him. The young sheriff turned his horse behind a low hillock, and scrambled quickly up the rise to an advantageous point from which he could see the approaching rider.

Except for the occasional glance along the valley, the man was intent upon his ride, which had an air of urgency about it, and Dan gained the impression that he did not want to be seen by anyone from the ranch in Roaring Valley.

When the horseman reached the bottom of the hillside, he was hidden from Dan's sight, but he could hear the man urging his horse up the hill. Suddenly, he burst over the top, bringing a gasp of surprise from Dan as he recognised Shorty Best.

Shorty eased himself in the saddle once he was back on Goddard's range, but he did not slacken the pace. He put his horse into a long steady gallop towards the Flying F, unaware that his ride was being watched.

As he watched Shorty ride away, Dan relaxed, and stroked his chin thoughtfully. From Matt Roberts' description, he knew that the Broken C range lay at the other side of Roaring Valley, and Dan wondered why Goddard's man had been over there.

He was puzzled as he returned to his horse, and rode across Roaring Valley to take a closer look at the Broken C. He kept to a steady pace until he reached a dip in the land where the ranch-house nestled in the hollow, close to a stream. Dan turned his horse below the skyline, slipped from the saddle, and crept to the edge of the hollow. He saw the long, low ranch-house stood a short distance away from the rest of the buildings grouped together near the corrals. There was no sign of activity, and after waiting a few moments, Dan was about to move away when two riders appeared over the edge of the hollow, a mile to his left. Dan watched them carefully as they rode at a gentle pace towards the ranch-house. Suddenly he stiffened.

'Goddard and his daughter!' he whispered to himself.

He let them almost reach the house before he slipped into the hollow and using every available cover, he hurried down the slope. He paused as Bill Goddard and Pat strode on to the veranda and knocked at the door, which he saw was opened by a young man who seemed pleased to see his two visitors. Once the door had closed behind them, Dan hurried forward, kept to the right of the house, and moved swiftly round the building to approach the back door cautiously. The door stood ajar, and seeing no one in the kitchen, Dan pushed the door gently open and stepped quickly inside. He crossed the room and moving further into the house, found himself in a spacious hall. Voices came from a room at the front, and Dan moved stealthily across the hall to halt close to the door.

'Wal, Pat, this is a surprise.' The voice was smooth. 'I always figured I'd win you in the end.'

'You can't be more pleased than I am, Stanton,' pointed out Goddard. 'It was only yesterday afternoon that I stopped Pat ridin' into Silverton; said she was goin' to marry this fellow Peters.'

'What made you change your mind, Pat?' asked Stanton curiously.

'I thought things over,' replied Pat quietly. 'I've known you a long time, and you always said you'd wait, so here I am.'

'This is a day to celebrate,' called Stanton. 'We must have a drink on this, and the wedding must be soon,' he added eagerly. 'Within the week.'

'But Russ, I can't be ready,' protested Pat.

'There's nothin' to get ready,' laughed the rancher. 'I'll marry you as you are. I'll ride into Silverton this afternoon and fix everythin'.'

Dan heard the glasses being refilled, and was about to move away, when Goddard spoke.

'I see thet havin' water rights from McLane has made a big difference to you using the east side of your range.'

'It sure has,' replied Stanton.

'You moved in there quickly,' continued Goddard, 'after McLane had outsmarted us both.'

Stanton laughed. 'I was frightened you might move in first,' he replied.

'I can tell you I was mighty sore about it,' said Goddard. 'I was prepared to make a fight for it, but Pat calmed me down. Wal, Stanton, now you've got her, maybe you won't object to your father-in-law sharing the water rights?'

'Now, Mister Goddard, it isn't up to me,' replied Stanton, doubtfully. 'It's really Clem McLane to say.'

'I know he has the final word,' said Goddard, 'but I'm sure if you said you were prepared to share, he wouldn't object, especially as he'll be able to charge me as well as you. I reckon you could put in a good word.'

'Wal, I don't know I've all that influence,' replied Stanton. 'However,' he added, after a moment's pause, 'I'll see what I can do.'

'Good,' answered Goddard with pleasure in his voice, 'then all is settled. We will...'

The rest of Goddard's words were lost on Dan as he felt the hard muzzle of a Colt press sharply against his back.

'All right,' snapped a voice behind him. 'What you snooping at?'

Dan straightened slowly and raised his arms. He glanced over his shoulder and saw a tall, fair haired, broad-shouldered cowboy standing close to him.

The man pushed Dan towards the door with his gun. 'In there!' he snapped.

Dan opened the door and the three occupants turned to stare in amazement as the young sheriff was escorted into the room, by the Broken C foreman.

'What's this, Jed?' snapped Stanton, annoyed by the intrusion.

'Caught him snoopin' in the hall,' explained Jed.

'You again,' gasped Goddard, hardly able to believe his eyes.

Stanton looked sharply at the older man. 'You know him?' he asked.

'He rode into Silverton yesterday, name's McCoy, and has been crossin' my path ever since,' explained Goddard who went on to tell Stanton of the happenings of the previous day.

'What you nosin' around here fer?' asked Stanton, turning to Dan.

Dan looked coolly at the dark haired young rancher. 'Information,' he answered icily.

'About what?' snapped Stanton.

'That's my business,' replied Dan.

'If it's the killer of Cal Smithson, then you won't find him here,' snarled Stanton. His face hardened as he warned Dan.

'If you take my advice you'll get on your way; we've a perfectly good sheriff to look after our affairs, besides, I don't like strangers prying around the Broken C.' He paused, and looked at Jed, a grin breaking slowly across his face. 'Jed, I figure you'd better show our friend what happens to meddlin' strangers around here.'

Jed grinned. 'Sure thing, boss.' He poked Dan with his gun. 'Outside, you,' he snapped.

Dan tensed himself at Stanton's words. He turned to the door, but with it half open he paused and looked at the immaculately dressed rancher.

'Stanton,' he said quietly but forcefully, 'it's strange coincidence, Cal Smithson and John Denston died the same way – a bullet in the back!'

For a fleeting moment he saw a flicker of astonishment cross Stanton's face, but it vanished quickly as the young man laughed.

'Why tell me?' he called.

Without waiting for him to answer, Jed pushed Dan roughly into the hall, and then propelled him further towards the front door. Dan staggered forward, and as he crashed into the door, he twisted the knob sharply and jerked the door open. In a flash Dan jumped outside, slamming the door behind him. Jed, taken by surprise at Dan's swift action, leaped across the hall, flung open the door and lunged outside. Amazement crossed his face when he saw that no one was in sight. He half turned, and in so doing, missed the full force of the blow, as

Dan jumped from the right hand side of the doorway, crashing his Colt on Jed's head. The Broken C man sprawled forward, and Dan leaped past him, jerked the reins of Bill Goddard's horse from the rail, jumped into the saddle, and sent the animal into a fast gallop.

Jed twisted on the veranda, his senses fading fast; he lifted his Colt and summoning his remaining strength squeezed the trigger. The bullet flew harmlessly into the ground, but the roar of the Colt brought Stanton and Goddard running from the house.

Stanton jerked to a halt when he saw the unconscious form of Jed, and the fleeing figure of Dan crouched low in the saddle. His Colt leaped to his hand and he loosed off two shots in Dan's direction, but the range was too great to be effective.

The sound of the gunfire brought two cowboys, who had returned to the ranch with Jed, running from the bunkhouse.

'Grab your horses,' yelled Stanton, as he leaped on to Pat's horse.

He pulled the animal round and the two cowboys closed in alongside him as they shoved the horses into an earth pounding gallop in pursuit of Dan.

## Chapter Six

As Dan thundered away from the Broken C he glanced anxiously over his shoulder, and seeing the three men leaping into their saddles, urged his animal to greater efforts. Dust swirled as he turned sharply round the end of the corrals and headed across the hollow. He pushed the horse hard up the slope and was relieved to see his black quietly champing the grass when he broke over the ridge.

The horse looked up, startled by the thundering hoofs, but Dan shouted a soothing word and the powerful animal snorted when it recognised Dan's voice.

The young sheriff pulled hard on the reins, but was out of the saddle before the horse stopped. He leaped to his own mount, jumped into the saddle, and sent the black away in an earth tearing gallop.

Although Dan had changed horses swiftly, the brief halt had enabled Stanton and his sidekicks to gain a few yards on Dan. Stanton's yell of triumph at seeing the gap narrowed froze on his lips when he saw Dan's new mount, and recognised a strong powerful horse which would have the stamina to out-run them. Desperately, the three men quirted their horses to greater speed, and as they gained on Dan, they pulled their Colts from their holsters. Colts roared behind him, and Dan flattened himself as bullets whined close to his head. He pushed the black harder, and the powerful animal stretched itself into an earth pounding gallop. As Dan drew away from his pursuers the firing became more spasmodic, and ceased altogether, but the three men hung grimly on to Dan's trail.

Dan regretted that he did not know the countryside better, and he realised that his only chance was to outrun Stanton and his sidekicks. Earth flew under the hoofs and, as the rough country above Roaring Valley came in sight, he knew he had a chance to outwit Stanton.

He hit the broken range at great speed, and twisted his way quickly between the hillocks, hoping to shake off the pursuit, but without success. Dan thundered between two low hills, and suddenly found himself on the edge of a steep drop into Roaring Valley. He checked his horse momentarily, and then, without further hesitation, sent the black over the edge, slithering and sliding down the rough slope. For one brief moment, he felt the horse falling, but by skilful riding both man and animal reached the bottom safely amidst a shower of stones and earth. He glanced anxiously over his shoulder and saw Stanton pause on the skyline of the ridge above.

Dan kicked his horse into a fast gallop and turned it towards the head of the valley. Stanton watched whilst his two sidekicks pulled alongside him.

'If he gits up there we've got him cornered,' he yelled, and shoved his horse forward down the slope.

The two men followed, but one was too eager, spurring his horse when it faltered. The animal lost its footing and, screaming with fright, rolled over and over down the hillside. Horse and rider crashed to the bottom amidst a cloud of dust, and lay in a huddled heap.

Stanton hauled on the reins and brought his horse to a sliding halt. He leaped from the saddle to find that the man was unconscious, but the horse was dead.

'Curley, look after Red,' he yelled, as the other rider pulled up in a swirl of dust.

The young rancher swung swiftly on to his horse and kicked it forward in pursuit of Dan.

As he pounded along the valley McCoy glanced back to see Stanton leave the fallen man, and continue the pursuit alone.

'Must want me out of the way pretty badly,' muttered Dan to himself, and urged his horse faster along Roaring Valley.

He reached the river, but finding the current too strong, he turned his horse along the bank and headed further up the valley. A great roaring filled the air, and as he galloped round a bend, Dan saw a waterfall leaping from the ground half way up the end of the valley, the sides of which steepened sharply and swung to meet a mile ahead. Desperately, Dan looked round for some means of escape as Stanton relentlessly pursued him, but he realised that his only chance lay up the rough slope at the end of the valley.

Russ Stanton eased himself in the saddle. He grinned confidently as Dan moved further along the valley. This stranger, who linked the deaths of John Denston and Cal Smithson, was trapped. Stanton drew his Colt, ready for when the rider turned to make a stand. Suddenly, the rancher started when he saw Dan send his horse up the steep, stoney slope. Spray from the pounding waterfall sent a thin veil across the scene as Stanton yelled, spurring his horse faster.

Dan glanced round anxiously, realising that his progress was now so slow that Stanton would soon be within shooting range. The roar of the waterfall on his right made his horse nervous, but when Dan whispered encouragingly in its ear, the broad-chested animal responded and carefully picked its way amongst the rocks.

A Colt roared behind him, and as the bullet whined close to him, Dan slid quickly from the saddle, slapping the black, to send it up the tricky slope.

The young sheriff dropped behind a boulder, drew his Colt from its holster, and took careful aim. Stanton had reached the bottom of the slope when Dan slid from his horse and his yell of triumph froze on his lips when he suddenly realised that Dan had the drop on him from above. He dived from the saddle a fraction of a second before Dan fired, and the bullet whistled harmlessly past him.

Dan loosed off two more shots quickly before scrambling round some rocks to a position a few yards higher. He was glad to see that his horse, relieved of his weight, had nearly reached the top of the slope and as he lay behind the rocks he surveyed the ground, planning his way to the top. Although there was plenty of cover, Dan realised the climb would not be easy, and there were several points where he would be exposed to Stanton's fire, but his biggest and immediate problem was to reach the next group of rocks fifteen yards to his left.

All was quiet below him and Dan peered cautiously round the side of the rocks. He ducked back quickly as a Colt crashed sending a bullet ricocheting off the rock above Dan's head. The young sheriff waited a few moments before he inched his way forward and peered round the rock once more, to bring a shot from Stanton. Dan ducked back again, but as the bullet whined past he jumped forward, sending two shots in Stanton's direction. Almost in the same movement he sprang forward, racing for the shelter of the next group of rocks. His shots held Stanton momentarily behind his cover and Dan had covered half the distance before the rancher looked upwards. Immediately he saw Dan his Colt sprang to life. Bullets crashed at Dan's feet and hit the hillside above his head. As Dan flung himself forward desperately to find the safety of the rocks, he felt a sharp pain in his right forearm. He hit the ground hard behind the cover and lay gasping for breath. He rolled over slowly and examined his arm. A long gash, caused by a bullet, was bleeding, but it was no more than a flesh wound. He pulled a large handkerchief from his pocket and bound the wound tightly before scrambling up a section of the slope which was not exposed to Stanton's gun.

The roar of the water hid all sound that both men might make on the rocks and at times they merely guessed where the other was. As Dan crouched behind some rocks, waiting for a chance to move, he heard bullets hit the ground some distance to his right. Quickly he glanced round the edge of his cover, and caught a glimpse of Stanton thirty yards below him. He fired swiftly and saw Stanton jerk round, clasping his leg as he fell behind the group of boulders. Seizing the opportunity, Dan scrambled upwards and moved a considerable distance before a bullet whistled past his head. He flattened himself to the ground and glancing back down the slope he saw Stanton peering from behind the boulders. Dan grinned to himself when he realised that the shot in the leg was preventing Stanton from following him. He holstered his gun, and moved quickly to the top of the slope, undamaged by the few desperate shots which the rancher sent after him.

As he reached the range at the head of Roaring Valley, Dan saw his horse was standing a few yards away. He gathered the reins quickly, patted the animal's neck affectionately, and swung into the saddle.

It was close on noon when Dan rode into Silverton. His arm throbbed as he slipped from the saddle and strode into the sheriff's office.

'Wondered where you'd got to,' greeted Matt Roberts. His smiles vanished quickly when he saw Dan's bound arm: 'What's happened?' he asked anxiously.

'Bullet grazed it,' explained Dan. 'Nothin' much really.'

'Better let the doc see it,' advised Matt. 'C'm on, I've just seen him go into his surgery.'

Matt hurried the dust-covered Dan across the street, and Doc Evans soon cleaned and bandaged Dan's wound.

'It will be all right,' he told them. 'Be a bit stiff for a day or so, but that's all.'

As the two men left the surgery, Matt paused on the sidewalk.

'I was just goin' to hev some dinner when you arrived,' he said. 'Guess you'll be ready for some?'

Dan nodded. 'I'll go an' clean up an' join you in ten minutes.'

Over their meal Dan told Matt about his brush with Stanton. The sheriff listened without interrupting and when Dan finished Matt rubbed his chin thoughtfully.

'You know,' he said, 'Stanton seemed mighty keen to get you out of the way.'

'Thet's what I figured,' agreed Dan. 'I don't think he'd hev worried so much about a prowler. I reckon I hit somethin' near the mark when I mentioned Denston an' Smithson being shot in the back.'

'Maybe you did,' mused Roberts. 'But provin' Stanton had anythin' to do with those killings is another thing.'

'We'll jest hev to wait for his next move,' said Dan. 'Maybe he'll overplay his hand,' he added. 'I'm goin' to take a closer look at Roaring Valley this afternoon, but first I think we ought to see what Lance Peters has to say.'

'We can't,' replied Matt. 'Lance Peters is out of town, I checked this morning. He's on a job way north, on the Kansas border. Likely to be away over a week.'

Dan whistled in surprise. 'Well, well, thet's convenient for Mister Stanton, there's no chance of Peters talkin' Pat Goddard out of marryin' Stanton!'

## Chapter Seven

Stanton cursed loudly when he saw Dan escape over the ridge at the head of Roaring Valley. His wound throbbed, and pulling a handkerchief from his pocket, he bound it tightly, stopping the flow of blood. His face was dark with anger as he pushed himself to his feet and stumbled down the slope towards his horse.

The leg pained him, and he felt weak from the loss of blood. Twice he fell, and only saved himself from rolling down the rocky incline by grasping protruding rocks which scarred and cut his hands.

Reaching his horse, he pulled himself into the saddle and sat for a few moments mustering his strength before sending the animal across the valley towards the place where he had left his sidekicks.

Curley and Red were not in sight when Stanton reached the dead horse, so he pushed his mount up the rough ground out of the valley. The animal struggled under the hot sun, and as Stanton's wound throbbed more, his temper became shorter and he cursed the horse louder for its slow pace. The going was easier once they were out of Roaring Valley, and after twisting his way through the rough hillocks on to the range, he saw his men some distance ahead.

When Curley heard the sound of hoofs behind him, he pulled his horse to a halt and waited for his boss to reach them. As Stanton pulled up alongside, Curley noticed the blood-stained handkerchief around his leg.

'You all right, boss?' he asked anxiously.

Stanton nodded. 'Not too bad,' he replied, 'but thet hombre got away. How's Red?'

'Leg broken,' answered Curley, 'lost a lot of blood, keeps passing out.'

'Git him on my horse an' I'll take him back. You ride into town fer the Doc,' ordered Stanton.

The two men struggled with the unconscious Red, and when they had got him on to Stanton's horse, the rancher mounted behind him. Curley swung in to his saddle and headed for Silverton at a dust stirring gallop, whilst the two wounded men rode for the Broken C at a steady pace. It was a hard struggle for Stanton to stop the unconscious man from slipping to the ground, and it was somewhat of a relief when the ranch-house came into view.

Concern showed on the faces of Bill Goddard and Jed Roscoe as they ran forward to meet him when he turned the end of the corrals.

'What happened?' asked Goddard as they eased Red from the horse.

Stanton scowled angrily. 'Red took a nasty fall, his horse was killed, an' his leg is in a bad way. Curley stayed with him an' I went after McCoy. Thought I had him cornered up Roaring Valley, but he nicked me an' I couldn't follow him.'

Goddard and Roscoe carried Red to the bunkhouse.

'Curley's gone for the Doc,' called Stanton. 'You all right, Jed?'

'Yeah,' shouted Roscoe, 'but I'd sure like to git my hands on thet lawman.'

Stanton grinned and rode to the ranch-house where Pat Goddard came down from the veranda and helped him from his horse.

'You all right?' she asked, but her voice lacked enthusiasm.

Stanton smiled. 'A lot better now I've seen you,' he replied smoothly.

Pat helped him into the house where she cut the blood-stained trousers around the wound and bathed it with hot water.

Curley soon returned with Doc Evans, who, after setting Red's leg, quickly attended to Stanton's wound.

'It's not too bad,' said the doctor, 'but really you should be in bed for a couple of days.'

'Can't,' snapped Stanton, irritated by all the fuss. 'I've a weddin' to fix up.'

'We can postpone it for a week or so,' said Pat, inwardly pleased for some excuse to postpone the event.

'No, no, we can't; we must get this over quickly,' protested Stanton. 'It's too good to be true that you've reconsidered and at last accepted one of my many proposals. If we wait, you might change your mind again.'

'Don't you two worry,' smiled Goddard. 'I'll see to everything. If Russ will lend us some horses, we'll ride back to town with Doc an' get the weddin' fixed fer two days time.'

'Fine,' smiled Stanton. 'Tell Jed to get you two horses, an' ask him to come in here when he's fixed you up.'

Doc Evans and Bill Goddard said goodbye, and strode from the room, but Stanton held out his hand to delay Pat.

'Aren't you goin' to kiss your future

husband goodbye?' he whispered smoothly.

Pat bent over Stanton, who was laid on the sofa, and kissed him lightly on the cheek. He grasped her by the wrists and pulled her towards him. His face hardened.

'I'm no fool, Pat,' he hissed. 'I know it's Lance Peters you want, an' you've been putting on an act in front of the others. Why you've changed your mind I don't know, maybe your father's made you. Whatever it is, I don't care, I'll have you as you are; you'll grow to love me.' He paused, but Pat did not speak. 'As fer Lance Peters, you can fergit him, he's on a wild goose chase up north, won't be back fer over a week. Fixed by me,' he added with a grin. 'I was determined to have him out of the way an' make one last bid fer you, but you beat me to it.' He pulled Pat hard against himself, and kissed her passionately. Pat tensed herself, but slowly relaxed, although her lips did not return his kiss. Slowly, he let her go. 'Your father will be waitin', Pat.' A grin spread across his face. 'Make sure you kiss better than that in two days' time.'

Pat's eyes were cold as she looked straight at Stanton.

'I hope our marriage will stop any chance of trouble developing over the two ranches,' she said icily. Her frock swished, as she hurried from the room, slamming the door behind her.

Stanton smiled to himself. 'Fiery red-head,' he whispered, 'I'll tame you.' His thoughts were interrupted by a knock on the door. 'C'm in,' he shouted.

'Congratulations, boss,' said Roscoe with a grin as he entered the room.

Stanton nodded his acknowledgment. 'Pour a couple of whiskeys,' he said, indicating the bottle on the big sideboard.

'I suppose this makes everythin' straightforward?' said Roscoe, pouring out the spirit. 'The two ranches will be yours.'

'I can't wait. I want the Flying F now,' snapped Stanton. 'Goddard isn't all that old.' He took the glass from his foreman.

'Accidents do happen,' smirked Jed evilly.

'We'll do it without a killin' if possible,' replied Stanton. 'We'll work as planned. Clem McLane has been bringin' in a few of the boys he knew up in Missouri.'

'Yeah, there's been a few strangers in town,' confirmed Roscoe. 'What about this tin-star thet's snoopin' around?'

'I reckon he can be fixed,' grinned Stanton. 'Give me a hand Jed we'll ride out to see Clem.'

Dan McCoy and Matt Roberts climbed into the saddles and turned their horses along the main street of Silverton. The afternoon was hot, and the few people who lingered on the sidewalks took no notice of the two men who left town by the east road. They rode slowly, their horses' hoofs scarcely flicking the dust, and twisted their way through the hills which formed the northern edge of the Flying F range.

Dan judged they had been riding for about an hour when they heard the pound of hoofs behind them. Matt looked round sharply, glanced at Dan, and with one accord they turned their horses off the trail and hid behind some huge boulders. They had scarcely reached their hiding place when three men appeared riding at a fast pace. Dan and Matt watched them carefully, and waited until they had disappeared round a bend in the trail before they pushed their horses forward.

'Know them?' asked Dan.

Matt shook his head. 'No,' he replied. 'We get a lot of strangers through Silverton.' He paused thoughtfully. 'It's a funny thing, though,' he added, 'I reckon there's been more around this last week or so an' some not in a hurry to move on.'

'Seen any out here recently?' queried Dan.

'No,' replied Matt. He looked at his young companion, curiously. 'What you gettin' at?'

Dan frowned. 'Thet's just it, I'm not sure, but I'm uneasy about the whole thing. Those hombres looked a no-good lot, they rode as if they were certain of the way, an' knew what they were about.'

'C'm on then,' answered Matt, 'let's see where they go.'

The two lawmen kicked their horses into a long steady lope, and were soon swinging round the hills to drop into Roaring Valley.

'There they are,' called Dan, pointing to a small dust cloud which swirled along the valley.

'Headin' fer the Walking A,' observed Matt.

'Wonder if they know Clem McLane?' mused Dan.

The two lawmen rode a further mile before Matt pulled his horse to a halt.

'I figure we'd be better keeping away from the ranch-house, at least fer the time being,' he said.

Dan nodded. 'Guess so,' he agreed.

'We'll head fer thet hill,' said Matt, indicating a small rise some distance across the valley. 'It gives a good view of the valley, you'll be able to get the lie of the land and we'll be fairly near the house.'

The two men sent their horses away from the trail, and as they headed across the lush grassland, Dan realised that it was superb grazing, much better than the neighbouring parts of both the Flying F and the Broken C.

When they reached the top of the shrub covered hill, they swung from the saddles, and after Dan had removed his spyglass from its cover, they lay down in a position from which they could keep the house under observation.

'Seems to be a lot of activity over there,' remarked Dan, passing the spyglass to Roberts.

Matt looked carefully at the buildings. 'Three horses outside the house,' he pointed out. 'Could be those hombres we saw back yonder.'

'Yeah,' agreed Dan. 'And it looks as if four more are joinin' them.'

'Where?' gasped Roberts, dropping the glass from his eye.

Dan pointed to a dust cloud, which moved steadily along the trail close to the foot of the hill forming the western edge of the valley. Roberts raised the glass and drew the men into focus.

'They're hard to make out, but strangers again I'd say,' remarked Matt.

'I'd sure like to know what's goin' on down there,' said Dan.

'Bit risky to move in there with all that activity,' continued Roberts.

'Guess you're right,' agreed Dan. 'Denston sure knew a good place when he saw one,' he observed as he looked round the valley.

'Yeah,' replied Matt. 'An' McLane doesn't make the best use of it; he could run far more head of cattle on it with this lush grass an' ample water supply – no fear of a drought.'

Suddenly, Dan grasped Matt's arm, and pointed to two riders to the south who were crossing the valley at a steady pace.

'Looks as if they've come down from the Broken C range,' observed Dan.

Roberts trained his glass on the two men. 'They sure have,' he said excitedly. 'It's Stanton an' his foreman.'

Dan let out a low whistle and the lawmen watched the two riders crossing the valley. They swung off the trail and turned down a dusty road which led to the Walking A.

'There must be a mighty important meeting goin' on down there,' observed Dan, as the two riders dismounted and entered the low wooden ranch-house.

'I'd like to...' The words froze on Matt's lips. He inclined his head, listening intently. Dan glanced sharply at the sheriff; he too had heard the noise on the hillside behind them. Both men scrambled quickly but quietly into the cover of some shrubs, and had only just got out of sight when two cowboys appeared over the edge of the hill.

'Told you there were two horses up here,' said the swarthy cowboy with the torn shirt.

'Guess we'd better find who owns them,' replied his thin-faced companion grimly.

The two men drew their Colts and started to move cautiously across the top of the hill, their eyes probing everywhere. Dan signalled to Matt, and when the cowboys were almost on top of them, the lawmen leaped from their hiding place, flinging their arms around the men's waists to drag them crashing to the ground.

Dan released his hold, rolled over quickly, turned, and as the startled cowboy struggled to get up, smashed his fist into the man's face. His head jerked backwards and crashed against a stone. A low moan escaped from the man's lips and he lay still. Dan spun round to go to help Matt, but he saw the sheriff dealing effectively with the thin-faced cowboy.

'You all right?' called Dan, hurrying over to Matt.

Matt nodded as he slapped the dust from his clothes. 'Yes thanks, but I figure we'll hev to move from here.'

'Sure,' agreed Dan. 'We may as well head fer town. We can't do much here an' there's too many over at the ranch-house fer it to be healthy.'

The two sheriffs had ridden far across the valley before the thin-faced cowboy began to regain consciousness. He sat up, shaking his head, trying to clear it. He turned, looking around the hill top until his eyes focused on the still form of his companion. He pushed himself to his feet and staggered over to the unconscious cowboy. As his head cleared, he saw the nasty gash on the man's head, and without wasting another moment hurried down the hillside to their horses. He brought them to the top of the hill quickly, slung his companion across the saddle of his horse, and was soon riding into the Walking A.

Cowboys ran to meet him and as soon as they had relieved him of the unconscious man, he hurried over to the ranch-house.

'C'm in,' a voice called, in answer to his knock on a door inside the hall. The thin-faced man entered the room to find it crowded. His boss was talking to Russ Stanton and he recognised Jed Roscoe, but the other seven were strangers.

'Hello, Charlie,' greeted McLane. 'What's the trouble?'

'Zeke an' I hev jest had a brush with the sheriff,' replied Charlie.

'What!' gasped McLane, his face clouding with annoyance. 'What happened?'

Charlie told his story quickly.

'Who was this other hombre?' snapped McLane.

'Don't know, boss,' replied Charlie. 'Didn't git much of a look at him, but I glimpsed a tin star just as Sheriff Roberts hit me.'

'A lawman?' said McLane, puzzled by Charlie's revelation.

'Think I can answer thet one,' broke in Russ Stanton, leaning forward in his chair. 'He's a stranger around here, name of McCoy,' he continued. 'This is his doin',' he added, pointing to his wounded leg.

'But what's he snoopin' around fer?' queried McLane.

'Seems thet Cal Smithson of the Flying F

was shot whilst talkin' to McCoy,' explained Stanton, 'an' he seems to want to know why.'

'Wal,' drawled Clem, 'I figure he's been around long enough. This is up your street,' he added, looking at one of the seven men.

The man nodded, and grinned, but before he could speak Stanton protested.

'No,' he said. 'They mustn't be seen too much around town.'

Roscoe jumped to his feet. 'I've a score to settle with thet hombre,' he said with venom. 'I'll fix him.'

Stanton grinned. 'He's yours, Roscoe, you take care of him.' He turned to the seven strangers. 'You boys hed better lay low here. Our plan will go into action the day after tomorrow – my wedding day.'

## Chapter Eight

Sheriff Matt Roberts looked up from the papers he was studying. A man hurried past the office window and the light from the kerosene lamp splashed across his grim, determined features.

'Jed Roscoe!' Matt whispered.

He pushed his chair back and crossed to the window, from which he saw the shadowy form of the Broken C foreman stride off the sidewalk.

'Headin' fer the Golden Cage,' muttered Matt, 'an' after Dan's encounter…' He left the sentence unfinished, grabbed his Stetson, and hurried from his office.

Since arriving back in Silverton, Roberts and McCoy had spent the evening discussing the problems confronting them, and trying to piece events together. It was only ten minutes ago that Dan had gone to the Golden Cage, leaving Matt to finish some paper work.

Dan was deep in thought as he leaned on the bar, sipping a beer, and was unaware of the cowboy who had come to the counter close to him.

'McCoy!' Dan was startled by the voice. 'I've a score to settle with you!'

Dan turned sharply to see Jed Roscoe facing him, feet astride, a supercilious grin on his face. As he watched the Broken C foreman, Dan was aware that men were moving away from them, and that the noise of the saloon was gradually subsiding. The laughter of a dance-hall girl froze at the height of its shriek, and left a grim tension in the air as the two men faced each other.

'We don't like strangers snoopin' around the Broken C,' hissed Roscoe. 'So my advice to you is to git on your horse an' ride.'

Dan's eyes narrowed. 'I don't take orders from you,' he said quietly, but firmly. 'I'll please myself when I leave this town.'

'You won't,' snapped Roscoe, ''cos I'm seein' thet you leave now.' He swept a glass of beer from the counter and in the same movement flung the contents into Dan's face.

Dan gasped, his hands flying to his face, but before he realised what was happening, Roscoe leaped forward and crashed his fist into Dan's mouth, sending him reeling backwards. The young sheriff would have fallen to the floor had he not grasped at the counter. He pulled himself upright and slowly wiped the trickle of blood from the corner of his mouth. His eyes darkened as he stared at the Broken C foreman.

'I aren't leavin' town until I'm ready,' he hissed.

'You are,' snarled Roscoe. His hand flashed to his holster and, like lightning, his Colt leaped into his hand, but Dan was faster and before Roscoe could press the trigger, the gun was sent spinning from his hand.

Roscoe, eyes widening with incredulity, stared at McCoy, amazed by the speed of Dan's draw.

A grim smile played around Dan's lips. 'You won't tell me what to do,' he hissed.

'Hold it!' a voice rasped authoritatively behind McCoy.

Dan gasped. He recognised Matt Roberts' voice, and was amazed that the sheriff had interfered. Slowly he looked round, and a grin spread across his face when he saw the startled look on Shorty Best's face as the sheriff pressed a cold Colt into his back.

'Thanks, Matt,' called Dan, realising that the sheriff had arrived in time to stop Shorty drawing on him from behind.

Matt relieved Shorty of his gun and pushed him forward towards the bar.

'Want me to clap them in jail, McCoy?' asked Matt.

Dan shook his head.

'All right, you two, out,' Matt snarled, motioning towards the door with his gun. 'An' don't trouble McCoy again.'

As the two men slunk from the saloon, the buzz of conversation grew louder; men and girls flocked back to the bar, and normal saloon life returned.

Dan called for two beers. 'How did you come to be there?' he asked curiously.

'Roscoe passed my office,' replied Matt. 'Looked as if he was up to no good an' when I saw him head fer the Golden Cage, I figured I'd better come along.'

'Mighty glad you did,' grinned Dan.

'An' a good job I stayed near the door, or Shorty would hev hed the drop on us both,' pointed out Matt. 'It was obvious he was there in case anything went wrong. You know it's queer thet a Broken C an' Flying F man should be in thet together.'

Dan rubbed his chin thoughtfully. 'Could Shorty be playin' a double game?' he asked. 'Don't forgit I saw him comin' off Broken C range.'

Matt frowned. 'It's possible,' he replied.

'An' Stanton visits McLane at the same time as strangers,' mused Dan. 'Only person whose out of thet little set up is Goddard. Could be they're plannin' somethin' he won't like.'

Matt looked curiously at Dan. 'But Stanton's goin' to marry Goddard's daughter.'

Dan frowned. 'Thet's what I can't figure out,' he said. He paused, looking at his beer thoughtfully before he continued. 'Stanton an' McLane are in this together; suppose Stanton put McLane up to gettin' Roaring Valley, an' the Valley really belongs to Stanton, then, he only needs the Flying F to...'

'Thet would make him the most powerful rancher around these parts,' interrupted Matt excitedly, 'an' thet'll come to him through marryin' Pat.'

Dan nodded. 'But what made Pat change her mind so quickly?' he asked thoughtfully.

Matt shook his head. 'I don't know. If we could pin the killin' of John Denston on McLane, we might smoke Stanton out.'

Dan drained his beer quickly. 'C'm on,' he said. 'I'd like to see Anne again.'

The two men hurried from the saloon and found Anne closing the cafe for the night. When all was locked up Anne made the two men a cup of coffee, and as they sat drinking it, Dan turned to Anne.

'I'm sorry to ask you about your husband's death,' he said, 'but it might help if you could recall anythin' peculiar about the night your husband was shot.'

Anne did not reply for a moment. Her eyes stared unseeingly at the cup in her hand. As she recalled the tragic night her voice was scarcely above a whisper.

'John had gone up the valley to check a herd with the night riders. The other boys were in town, and I was alone at the house. He told me what time he would be back and when he knew I was alone he was never late. When he didn't ride in I got anxious, and as I had no one to send I went out myself.' Anne paused. Her lips trembled. 'I found him two miles from the house.'

'I'm sorry, Anne, to keep on,' said Dan, 'but did you notice anythin' peculiar?'

Anne shook her head. 'No, I don't think so,' she answered quietly.

Dan eased himself in his chair. 'Wal, Matt,' he said disappointedly, 'there's nothin' to go on there.'

'Wait a minute,' said Anne sharply, her eyes widening as if she were trying to recall something. 'I don't suppose it's important,

93

but, when I left the house a light, as if a cowboy had struck a match, flickered on the hillside above the house.'

'Thet could hev...'

Matt's words were cut short as Anne continued excitedly. 'I can remember now, a similar light flickered just after I found John!'

Dan looked sharply at Matt.

'Anythin' else, Anne?' asked Matt.

'Well, I was too overwrought at the time,' replied Anne, 'but I recall thet when I got near the house a coyote whined just beyond the house and another answered not far from me.'

'Coyotes!' Matt gasped. 'But John told me he'd never seen any in the valley.'

Anne looked surprised. 'Thet's right,' she gasped. 'I'd forgotten that.'

'Signals,' said Dan. 'A put up job – why did your riders go to town thet night?'

Anne looked thoughtfully for a moment. 'Jed Roscoe had called a meeting of cowhands from the three ranches.'

'Was your husband in the habit of checking the night riders?' asked Dan.

Ann looked curiously at him. 'Yes,' she whispered.

Dan's eyes brightened. 'Stanton would

94

hev known this, and therefore would know you would be on your own.'

Matt gasped as he followed Dan's argument. 'He kills John knowing thet Anne will get uneasy an' probably look fer him – if she doesn't, then he was probably prepared to kill her too.'

'But what for? McLane got the ranch, not Stanton.'

'Put up by Stanton so as not to bring trouble from Goddard,' answered Dan.

Anne nodded. Her face was white, her eyes narrowed as she whispered with venom, 'Stanton! Russ Stanton!' Suddenly she looked up, her eyes flaming with hate. 'Get him, Matt! Get him!'

Matt jumped to his feet and putting his arm round her shoulder comforted her. 'Calm yourself, Anne, I know this has been a shock to you, but I've no proof.'

'Proof!' Anne cried. 'But what more…'

'We've only been theorising,' said Matt quietly. 'I can't arrest a man on that.'

'Matt's right,' said Dan. 'But we'll see you have your Roaring Valley back. Tomorrow I think I'll visit Clem McLane.'

Dan took his time riding along the edge of the Broken C range overlooking Roaring

Valley. He stopped frequently, studying the valley and the Flying F land through his spyglass. During the morning he noted a huge dust cloud swirling slowly on the Flying F range, and, at mid-day, he realised it had moved nearer the poorer ground above Roaring Valley.

'Stanton must hev persuaded – or told – McLane to let Goddard hev water rights,' mused Dan. 'He's soon on the move.'

Dan studied the valley closely throughout the day, but found nothing out of the ordinary. Life at the Walking A went on much as would be expected. It was late afternoon when he decided it was time to pay McLane the intended visit. He turned his horse, and paused on the edge of the slope. Suddenly, a rifle shattered the stillness, and almost in the same instance, Dan's head jerked backwards. His brain pounded, as an overwhelming blackness poured in. He swayed in the saddle, pitched forward, and slid round the horse's neck, to fall awkwardly to the ground on the edge of the slope. He rolled over and over, faster and faster, amidst a shower of stones and earth, until he reached the bottom, where he lay still, face upwards, arms outstretched.

A figure appeared on the edge of the hill.

He looked down at the still form, a grin spreading across his face as he pushed a rifle back into its holder.

'Clever Mister McCoy won't bother us any more,' he muttered with satisfaction.

Jed Roscoe turned his horse and headed for the Broken C.

## Chapter Nine

Matt Roberts toyed with his cup of coffee as he sat on a high stool beside the counter in Anne's Cafe. A worried frown wrinkled his forehead, and he stared unseeingly in front of him. Outside the shadows were lengthening and the chill wind of evening was blowing through the Texas town of Silverton.

Anne Denston finished serving a customer and walked over to Matt.

'I'm sure he'll be all right,' she said, jerking Matt back from his thoughts. 'Dan can take care of himself.'

The sheriff smiled faintly, knowing that there was no ring of confidence in Anne's voice, and that her words were merely an echo of a hope.

'Dan should hev been back before now,' muttered Matt. 'I can't help feelin' somethin's wrong.'

'I know how you feel,' answered Anne, 'but he could have got a lead on to something.'

'I suppose so,' said Matt. 'All the same I think I'll ride out to the Walking A, see what

McLane's got to say.'

'Wait a little longer,' replied Anne. 'I'm closing early, in an hour's time; wait until then. If Dan doesn't show up by the time you walk me home, then ride.'

'All right,' agreed Matt, but he spent an uneasy hour. He watched the door anxiously, and every time it opened, he looked with eager anticipation, but the hour passed without a sign of Dan.

As Anne turned from locking the door, she took Matt's arm. 'I'm sorry,' she whispered. 'Maybe I shouldn't have persuaded you to stay.'

Matt smiled reassuringly, and they hurried along the sidewalk.

Only the pale light from the stars relieved the darkness of the Texas countryside. A black horse stamped at the ground uneasily as it nuzzled the still form which lay at the bottom of the steep slope. Through the late afternoon and evening the horse had stayed near the man, moving round and round and pushing at the silent form, trying to find some life. A low frightened whinny came from the animal, it raised its head sharply, its ears upright, listening, but only the low moan of the soft breeze broke the silence of

Roaring Valley. The horse lowered its head slowly, and started to lick the man's face.

Five minutes passed before the animal was rewarded, when Dan's eyes flickered open with great effort. He lay staring upwards, his mind trying to comprehend his position. He could not understand the darkness, but gradually, he realised that it was night. Dan raised his arm slowly, the effort was almost too much for him, and he felt his head gently. He was startled to feel a deep furrow, and his hair matted with blood. The horse licked him again, and a faint smile broke on Dan's lips as he patted the horse.

With a struggle the young sheriff sat up; his head throbbed; the world spun in front of him. Breathing deeply he held his head in his hands until he was able to see things more clearly. Dan reached out, grasped his stirrup, and pulled himself to his feet. He felt weak, his legs wanted to fold up under him, but grimly he held on to the leather, leaning against his strong horse. He grasped his saddle, and summoning his strength he put one foot into the stirrup and slowly pulled himself upwards. Suddenly, his foot slipped and Dan dropped, only just saving himself from falling to the ground by grasping the stirrup. He leaned heavily against his horse, gasping for breath. As soon as he felt stronger Dan tried to mount his horse again, and, this time, he was successful. He dropped on to the saddle and hung on to it tightly, feeling that any relaxation of his grip would send him crashing to the ground. Nearly ten minutes passed before he reached for the reins, and put the black into a slow walk in the direction of Silverton.

How long he rode Dan never knew, but he was glad when he realised that he was riding past houses and had reached the town. Seeing a light burning in Anne's house he halted his horse and slid from the saddle. He pushed open the gate, staggered to the front door, and knocked loudly.

'Dan!' gasped Anne as the light from her lamp revealed her caller. 'Come in,' she added. 'We've been…'

She cut short her words when she saw Dan's legs begin to buckle. She grasped him firmly, and helped him inside. 'What's happened?' she asked anxiously, her eyes wide with concern.

Dan did not speak until Anne had helped him into a chair.

'Someone took a shot at me during the afternoon,' he said, bending his head forward.

Anne gasped when she saw the ugly wound. 'I'll get the doctor right away,' she said, picking up a shawl and draping it over her head and shoulders.

'Get Matt at the same time,' said Dan.

'I can't,' answered Anne. 'He's gone looking for you!'

Matt Roberts' face was grim as he rode out of Silverton by the east road. He had known Dan only a short time, but he liked the tall, slim, upright young man, and he swore vengeance on anyone who had harmed him.

Not knowing how much riding he would have to do before the night was out, he rode at a steady pace to conserve his horse's energy. The Texas countryside seemed peaceful as he rode along Roaring Valley, only the low moan of Walking A cattle broke the silence on his left, but on the hill top to his right the sound of cattle was louder.

'Bill Goddard must hev moved some of his cattle,' he mused.

Lights shone from the Walking A and noise came from the bunkhouse as Matt rode up to the main building. He slipped from the saddle and knocked on the door. Surprise showed on Clem McLane's face when he saw the sheriff.

'Wal, Sheriff Roberts,' he exclaimed. 'What do you want out here at this time of night?'

'A word with you, McLane,' answered Matt.

'C'm in,' offered McLane, stepping to one side. 'But I ain't broke the law,' he added as Roberts strode past him.

McLane closed the door, and led the sheriff to a room on the left-hand side of the hall. Matt felt that McLane had deliberately kept him away from the room on the right, and he thought his suspicions were confirmed when there was no fire in the room which was obviously not in use.

Matt came straight to the point. 'Dan McCoy, a friend of mine, said he would pay you a visit today,' he explained. 'He hasn't returned…'

'And you're worried,' grinned McLane, finishing Matt's sentence. 'Wal, we haven't seen him here,' he added. His smile faded. 'If he'd been here I couldn't hev guaranteed his safety after your treatment of my two riders.'

Matt stiffened. 'I could hev run those two hombres in,' he answered sharply.

'You shouldn't hev been snoopin' around the Walkin A,' snapped Clem. 'If you'd

103

finished with a bullet in you, you'd hev hed yourself to blame.'

'Is thet what's happened to McCoy?' snapped Matt.

'I've told you I haven't seen him,' replied McLane, his eyes smouldering with anger. 'Now you've got your answer, so hit the trail.' He walked across the room and opened the door.

As Matt reached the door, he stopped, and looked hard at McLane.

'A number of strangers around your place,' he said testily, 'see thet they keep on the right side of the law.'

McLane matched look for look. 'Friends from Missouri,' he replied. 'They haven't troubled you.'

'I'm jest warnin' you,' answered Matt, and left the house.

He was puzzled as he swung into the saddle and turned his horse away from the house. He felt that McLane was telling the truth, and yet, where was Dan?

He was passing the bunkhouse when the door opened and the shaft of light spilled across him. A cowboy stepped through the door and Matt recognised Charlie.

'Roberts!' the word was spat out with hate, and the man reached for his gun, but the sheriff was quicker. Charlie's gun was only half way out of its holster when Matt's bullet crashed into his shoulder. With a yell of pain the cowboy fell back against the doorpost.

Matt halted his horse. 'Don't draw on the Law again,' he snapped. His smoking gun still pointed in the direction of the doorway halting the Walking A riders as they ran to the door. The door of the ranch-house burst open and Clem McLane stopped suddenly against the rail when he saw Matt's Colt.

'McLane,' shouted Matt, 'keep your cowpokes under control or it'll be the worse fer you.' Without waiting for an answer the sheriff kicked his horse into a gallop and was lost in the darkness before McLane or his riders realised it.

He kept to a fast pace until he knew there was no pursuit. Deciding that he may as well question Stanton he turned his horse across Roaring Valley and headed for the Broken C.

When he reached the ranch he found that neither Stanton nor his foreman was there, and the four cowboys in the bunkhouse could give him no clue as to their whereabouts, but they were certain that no stranger had ridden to the Broken C that day.

Matt rode slowly away from the ranch, his

105

mind heavy with worry. He felt something was wrong, but there was nothing he could do now until daylight. Reluctantly he turned his horse back towards Silverton. He put the animal into a steady trot and they covered the mile quickly at an easy pace.

Matt was cutting through a group of low hills when he heard the sound of a buggy coming in the opposite direction. He pulled his horse off the trail and waited behind a group of rocks. The buggy rounded a bend in the trail at a slow pace, and as it approached, Matt made out the forms of a man and a woman. He steadied his horse and watched carefully as the buggy drew nearer.

'Stanton and Shirley Parker!' he gasped to himself. His brain pounded; thoughts raced as he watched the buggy moving along the trail. Stanton with another woman on the eve of his wedding! Shirley Parker, singer at the Golden Cage, who was thought to be Clem McLane's girl! Matt stiffened at the thought of the trouble which could blow up. What was Stanton's game? Could he use this information to force Stanton's hand? He was roused from his thoughts as he suddenly realised that the speed of the buggy had altered, and it was slowing down. As it came to a halt, Matt slipped from the saddle and moved quickly, but quietly, along the side of the trail. As the buggy and its occupants became more distinguishable, Matt crept curiously to the cover of some rocks close by.

'Stop worryin', Shirley, everythin' will work out right. I'm not desertin' you.' Stanton's voice was quiet.

'You'd better not, Russ,' replied the girl. 'After all we've planned, but it gives a girl a funny sensation to see her husband-to-be marryin' someone else tomorrow.'

'It will be for only a little while,' comforted Stanton.

The girl did not speak for a moment. Stanton drew her closer to him.

'Can't it be done some other way?' asked Shirley.

'This is the easiest,' replied Stanton. 'Married to his daughter, Goddard will see things my way. If he won't sell cheap then a little accident, and the Flying F will be mine. Marryin' Pat is jest a safeguard; if Goddard turns down my offer, wal, I could hardly marry her afterwards.'

'And what about Clem?' asked the girl. 'Weddings may be catching; he's sure to ask me. I've played him along long enough to keep him quiet for you.'

'His turn will come,' chuckled Stanton,

'and then all will be ours.' He pulled the girl towards him and kissed her passionately. As their lips parted, he flicked the reins. 'We can do this in comfort,' he laughed as the horse moved forward.

Matt straightened himself when the buggy had vanished into the darkness. For a few moments he stood staring after it, hardly able to believe what he had overheard.

## Chapter Ten

About the same time as Matt Roberts was turning his horse towards Silverton, Clem McLane strode on to the veranda of his house with a thin, wiry, hook-nosed cowboy.

'Watch the herd all night,' McLane instructed, 'an' report first thing in the mornin'.'

The man nodded, untied his horse from the rail, and rode up the spur behind the house on to the Flying F range. He could hear the low moan of the herd some distance to his right and it did not take him long to locate the cattle. He left his horse securely tied to a low shrub about a quarter of a mile from the herd and crept cautiously forward.

Casey grinned to himself when he saw that the Flying F cowboys had bedded down the cattle in a hollow, the rim of which formed a natural vantage point from which to watch the herd. Before settling down he scouted round and was taken aback when he saw there were a large number of riders with the herd. If Stanton's theory did not prove to be right, then their task tomorrow would be more difficult. Casey, however, was not one to worry about the future and he settled down to await the dawn.

The sky was paling in the east, and, in the faint light, Casey watched the Flying F men start another day. Suddenly he stiffened. A lone rider approached the opposite side of the hollow, paused on the rim, and rode slowly down to the camp.

Bill Goddard's foreman rode easily towards the eastern rim of the Flying F range. He smiled to himself when he thought how Goddard had anticipated a share in the water rights of Roaring Valley, and already a huge herd of his cattle were on the poorer ground on the eastern rim. But, today, only a few cowboys would remain with the herd; this was Pat Goddard's wedding day and her father insisted that as many of the hands as possible should be at the wedding celebrations. Dave Walters had the unenviable task of deciding who should stay. He tossed the names over in his mind as he rode towards lightness which was breaking the darkness of the eastern horizon.

When Dave rode into camp he was greeted by welcoming voices and the appetising smell of bacon, beans, and boiling coffee.

'It should only take five of you to watch the herd,' finished Walters, after he had explained the reason for his early call. 'I figure the best way is to cut the cards.'

A murmur of eager excitement, at the anticipation of a day in town, ran through the men as they crowded round the box on which Walters placed a deck of cards. There was a tense quietness in the air as each man drew his card and turned it face upwards. Groans and friendly chaffing passed between the men as the foreman signalled out the unlucky five, and the rest hurried to saddle their horses.

With excited whoops they rode out of the hollow and headed for the Flying F. Dave Walters paused on the rim of the hollow, and after looking back over the herd to see his men riding to take up their positions, he turned his horse to follow the other riders.

On the far side of the hollow a lone cowboy crept away from the rim and hurried to his horse.

Casey swung swiftly into the saddle and put his horse into a gallop towards Roaring Valley. He kept to a fast pace down the hillside, and was soon pulling up in a dust-raising halt in front of the Walking A, where he hurried inside the ranch-house.

'It's a cinch, Butch,' called Casey excitedly, as he burst into the room where McLane and the other six men from Missouri awaited his return. He gave them details of the lay-out.

'How many men with the herd?' asked Butch.

'Five,' grinned Casey. 'They've all moved out except five.'

Smiles broke across the faces of the men and Clem turned to Butch.

'Stanton was right,' he shouted. 'Goddard did pull his men out fer the weddin'.'

'This Stanton's a mighty persuasive fellow,' grinned Butch.

'Said he'd insist on all Flying F men being there if his men were goin'.'

'This leaves the way open nicely,' said McLane.

After Casey had detailed the lay-out of the hollow again, Butch outlined his plan quickly. When he was satisfied, he looked at McLane.

'Clem, you get yourself off to the wedding,' he said.

McLane started to protest, but Butch cut him short.

'It'll be better,' he insisted. 'Less suspicious if you are there.'

Clem looked thoughtful for a moment.

'Guess you're right,' he said. 'Charlie can ride with you instead. He knows the country like the back of his hand an' knows where we're hidin' the cattle.'

Butch realised that most people would be at the wedding and, wanting to minimise the chance of any interference, he had timed the jumping of the herd for ten-thirty. He had his men in the saddles in plenty of time and kept them to a walking pace as Casey led them towards the hollow.

'This place'll do nicely fer the horses,' said Butch, pulling to a halt a quarter of a mile from the herd. 'Charlie, stay with them, we'll hev a look at the herd.' He grinned, showing a row of uneven teeth, yellow from tobacco chewing.

Seven men slipped from the saddles, secured their horses, and moved off towards the hollow. The ground rose slightly towards the rim, and as they neared the edge of the hollow, Butch signalled his men to the ground. They crept forward cautiously until they were looking down upon the herd.

Butch studied the land carefully; he watched the Flying F men as they patrolled the herd, keeping on the slope a little above the steers in the hollow. A quarter of an hour passed before he grunted with satisfaction, and the men knew he had decided on his final plan.

'Five of us will take a man each,' he instructed quietly. 'I will fire first an' immediately, you all do the same. I want no mistakes, no one must escape. Then grab your horses and ride in on the herd. We hev to drive the cattle south, so the other two an' Charlie will be on the north side ready to ride in as soon as they hear the shots.'

The men nodded their understanding, and Butch delegated each one to his task. He signalled them away from the rim of the hollow, and they moved quickly, but quietly, back to their horses.

Half-an-hour passed before Butch gave the order to move out. He was the last to leave, but he was not long in reaching the rim of the hollow. He smiled grimly to himself as he eyed a red-shirted cowboy astride his horse immediately below him. The man idly rolled himself a cigarette as he relaxed in the saddle.

Butch glanced at his watch; twenty-five past ten. He reckoned the rest of the gang would be in position. He raised his rifle and drew the broad back of the cowboy into line. The shirt stood like a red blotch at the end of his sights. Slowly, he lowered the rifle, and stared at the minute hand of his watch. Excitement mounted in Butch. He loved action, and more so when there was good money at the end of it. He glanced at the cowboy, and then back to his watch, impatiently. It seemed an age before the minute hand moved on to ten thirty. As it did so, a cool calmness descended over the killer. He put his watch away slowly, picked up his rifle, and raised it to his shoulder. The red shirt came into his sights, and Butch gently squeezed the trigger. He was oblivious to the crash which was flung across the hollow as he saw the man on the horse jerk upright and stiffen, as if some great hand had slapped him on the back. Momentarily, the man stayed in that position, but as the horse, startled by the noise, jerked forward, he fell from the saddle.

Rifles crashed around the hollow.

Butch jumped to his feet, ran to his horse, and swung quickly into the saddle. He put his horse over the edge of the hollow and in a glance saw three men move in from the north, and four others appear astride their animals. The killer grunted with satisfaction; his men had done their job, and no Flying F men remained to bear witness.

The steers, frightened by the crash of the rifles, were already on the move. Those on the outside of the herd tried to turn inwards, but were pushed back bellowing. The uneasiness spread through the herd like a ripple on a pond until those on the north side turned from the pushing steers and made to move up the slope. Suddenly, they found three yelling cowboys riding down on them. The steers paused, and as the horses pounded dust in front of them, they turned back upon the herd. Steer crashed against steer, horns ripped into flesh, and cattle bellowed with fright and pain. Dust swirled, rising in a cloud above the hollow, as the cattle turned and spilled out of the centre of the bowl and ran round the slopes of the hollow in either direction, looking for some means of escape, only to find five more men riding down upon them.

Butch spurred his horse furiously, riding back and forth, yelling instructions as he sized up the situation. Skilfully, the cowboys kept the cattle under control and as two streams of steers raced round the hollow towards each other, the men neatly funnelled them together up the slope, and over the south rim of the hollow. When Butch saw that the cattle were moving out of the hollow in the right direction, he yelled to two of his men to follow him. They set their horses pounding up the slope alongside the cattle, and, once over the top they flattened themselves along the horses' backs, yelling for greater speed. Butch bit his lip anxiously when it seemed that he was not moving faster than the steers. If he wasn't careful the cattle could easily get out of control once they felt the freedom of the range, after the confines of the hollow. At all costs he must outride the herd and slow it down. His horse, muscles rippling, stretched itself across the grassland, and gradually began to overhaul the leading steers. His sidekicks kept pace with him and soon they were pounding alongside the leaders.

'Take the far side, Jim,' yelled Butch.

The cowboy spurred his horse faster, swung gradually across the front of the herd, and steadied his mount until the steers caught up with him. When Butch saw him in position he kicked his horse forward and turned it sharply across the front of the herd. Yelling and swearing, Butch rode back and forth, knowing full well that one false step by his horse meant certain death under thousands of pounding hoofs. His sidekicks applied pressure gently from each side, and gradually the pace slackened, and the cattle closed up into a more compact herd. When the pace satisfied Butch, he left the front of the herd and saw that his men had taken up their positions quickly.

He pulled his horse to a halt and stood in the stirrups, surveying the moving herd. Satisfied that all was well he slumped back into the saddle and was wiping his face with a large handkerchief when Charlie rode up.

'Nice work,' yelled Charlie, pulling his horse to a halt alongside Butch.

The killer grinned. 'Dealt with a few herds in my time,' he called, 'before I took to this,' he added, patting his Colt. 'How far do we keep on this run?'

'About five miles,' replied Charlie, 'then we start swinging westwards.'

'Westwards?' Butch puckered his brow as if he doubted the wisdom of taking that direction. 'But thet'll keep us on Flying F land!'

'Yeah,' answered Charlie. 'We take the cattle to a small secluded valley in the hills in the extreme south-west of Goddard's land.'

Butch looked startled. 'But…' His protestations were cut short by Charlie.

'None of the Flying F ever go there,' he re-assured the killer. 'Besides, Stanton figures thet Goddard will never expect the cattle to still be on his own land, and another thing, after Stanton gits the Flying F it won't be so far to move the cattle back, with a new brand, of course,' he added with a laugh.

Butch slapped his thigh and his surprised look changed to loud laughter. 'Wal, I'll be… I've sure got to hand it to Stanton.' He pulled his horse round. 'C'm on Charlie, lead the way.' The two men kicked their horses into a steady gallop and rode out in front of the herd.

## Chapter Eleven

Sheriff Matt Roberts had much to occupy his mind as he rode back to Silverton. Approaching Anne Denston's he suddenly stiffened in the saddle, his eyes widening with surprise.

'Dan's back!' he exclaimed when he saw the horse tied to the rails. Excitedly, he swung from the saddle and hurried up the path. A light still burned downstairs and Anne soon opened the door in answer to his knock.

'Matt!' she cried, relief showing in her voice at the sight of the sheriff. 'Oh! I'm so glad you're back.'

She stepped aside to let Matt in, but as she closed the door the sheriff sensed there was something wrong.

'What's the matter?' he asked anxiously. 'Is Dan all right?'

Anne nodded and led Matt into the kitchen. Quickly she told him about Dan's arrival.

'He must have been laid out there a long

time,' she concluded, 'and I was frightened for you.'

Matt smiled. 'That's sweet of you, Anne. What did the doctor say?'

'Well, the wound wasn't as bad as it appeared at first,' explained Anne, 'but Doc Evans says he should be in bed for a day at least to get over it. He's sleeping well now.'

Matt laughed. 'Dan's a strong boy an' I figure there'll be no keepin' him in bed tomorrow when he hears my news.'

Anne looked curiously at the lawman. Matt saw that her curiosity was roused. He gripped her by the shoulders and laughed.

'You'll have to wait, too,' he said. 'It's bed fer you, you look about all in.'

Anne started to protest but Matt halted her with a kiss.

'Good night,' he said. He turned to go, but stopped by the door. 'Would you like me to stay here tonight in case Dan needs anything?' he asked. 'I can sleep on two chairs in the same room. It will mean you can get a good night's rest without any worry.'

Anne smiled. 'Thanks,' she said. 'I'll get you some blankets.'

Matt awoke the following morning to the smell of a good breakfast frying in the kitchen below. He rolled out of the two chairs and stretched himself, driving the stiffness from his body. Dan was still sleeping soundly, but before Matt had finished dressing the young man stirred and slowly opened his eyes.

Matt crossed quickly to the bed. 'Hello, Dan,' he said quietly, a smile broadening across his face.

Dan stared at the sheriff, not recognising him for a moment. He looked round the room and then back at Roberts. A faint smile flicked his lips.

'Hi, Matt,' he whispered dryly. 'What happened? Where am I?' He struggled to sit up.

'You're all right, Dan,' replied Matt, pushing the young man back into the pillows. 'You're at Anne's. Take it easy until I bring you some breakfast.'

Dan smiled and nodded. Matt was fastening his gun belt when there was a knock on the door. The sheriff hurried across the room and opened the door, to find Anne with a breakfast tray.

'Morning, Matt,' she greeted cheerily. 'How's the patient?'

Matt took the tray from her. 'He'll be all right, Anne,' smiled Matt. 'He's had a good night and is jest gathering himself together.

122

This'll do him the world of good,' he added, indicating the breakfast.

Anne crossed the room and Dan turned his head to smile a greeting. 'Thanks, Anne, for everythin' you…'

'Think nothing of it, Dan,' Anne interrupted. 'I was only too glad to see you alive.'

'Anne, fetch your breakfast up here,' instructed Matt. 'Then you can hear what I have to tell Dan.'

Anne hurried downstairs and when she returned with another tray she found Dan sitting up in bed ready to enjoy his breakfast.

'Let's hear what happened to you first,' said Matt as the three friends started their meal.

Dan told his story quickly.

'So McLane was telling the truth, you never did get there!' mused Matt.

'Thet's right, an' I don't know who took a shot at me,' said Dan. 'Now, what's the news you hev?'

Matt smiled. 'Luck was more with me than it was with you,' he said, and went on to relate the happenings of the previous night. As his story unfolded, Dan and Anne stopped eating and stared at the sheriff in amazement.

'Someone should warn Pat Goddard,' gasped Anne as Matt finished his story.

'Thet was my first instinct,' replied Matt, 'but she wouldn't believe us, nor would Goddard; Stanton would deny it, as would Shirley. No, we've got to leave things as they are. We know Stanton's plans, but can't prove anythin'; we've jest got to be extra vigilant and hope Stanton makes a wrong move.'

Dan looked very thoughtful. 'If this Shirley is McLane's girl, or he thinks she is, maybe we could use it in an attempt to draw information out of McLane.'

'But he wouldn't believe it, especially when Stanton marries Pat,' pointed out Anne.

Dan nodded. 'But it might be a useful move in the future. Wal, I reckon we'd better go and see the weddin'.'

'The doctor says you are to spend the day in bed,' protested Anne.

'Bah, doctors!' called Dan. 'After thet meal I feel fine, an' you aren't keepin' me up here when there's a pretty bride to see.'

Anne and Matt laughed, and seeing Dan's determination, they agreed to let him get up.

The marriage of Pat Goddard was regarded in Silverton as a great event. Although the arrangements for the wedding had been rushed through, most of the townsfolk had declared this a holiday and by the time the three friends walked down Main Street the crowds had gathered.

'I think we'll try to get near the church,' suggested Anne.

The two men agreed, and the three friends threaded their way along the sidewalk through groups of smiling, chattering people. The crowd was thickest around the church, but, on Matt's suggestion, they stayed on the edge of the crowd on the roadway, so that they would have a good view along the street, and be close to the buggy when it stopped.

Excitement stirred through the crowd as half-past ten approached. People craned their necks as the steady clop of horses' hoofs heralded the approach of two riders. Jed Roscoe accompanied his boss Russ Stanton, who cut a fine figure in a black frock coat, black trousers, topped by a fancy waistcoat with a wide brimmed, low crowned, black sombrero covering his thick dark hair.

They pulled to a halt a few yards from Dan, and, as they swung from the saddles, Roscoe's glance met Dan's. For a fleeting moment surprise showed on Roscoe's face, but the expression was so quickly controlled that Dan doubted if he had interpreted the look correctly. As the two men walked up the path to the church the young sheriff, thoughtfully rubbing his chin, gazed after them.

'Roscoe seemed a little startled when he saw you,' commented Matt.

Dan looked at Matt sharply. 'You noticed it too?' he said.

'Maybe Roscoe threw thet bullet at you,' suggested Matt, 'an' didn't figure on seein' you again.'

Any further conversation was halted as the crowd along Main Street started cheering. People pushed forward, straining their necks to see what was happening.

Anne stepped into the roadway. A smile crossed her face and turning to the two lawmen she called excitedly. 'They're coming.'

The clop of a trotting horse grew louder as the buggy driven by Bill Goddard moved along Main Street, towards the church.

Dan watched the two occupants carefully as the buggy came to a halt close to him. Goddard smiled happily at the people around him, acknowledging their cheers and greetings. As he helped Pat from the Buggy

126

Dan studied her, and was certain that her smile was forced. He watched father and daughter enter the church before turning to Matt.

'Thet girl doesn't want to marry Stanton,' he said.

'But she said…' started Matt.

'I know what she said, but her eyes gave her away,' replied Dan. 'It was as if she regretted having to do something.'

'What do you mean, having to do it?' asked Anne. 'She could have turned Stanton down.'

'Maybe she couldn't,' answered Dan thoughtfully.

The crowds hung about until after the ceremony, and great cheering broke out when the bride and groom appeared on the steps of the church. The reception was held in some private room at the Golden Cage, but Bill Goddard was soon in the bar, proclaiming that all drinks were on him.

Goddard was joking with a group of townsfolk at one end of the bar when his foreman Dave Walters came up to him.

'I'm going out to check thet herd we just moved to east side,' he said.

'It'll be all right,' assured Goddard loudly. 'Stay here an' celebrate the union of the two biggest spreads out here.'

'Those cattle are on new ground, Mister Goddard,' replied Walters crisply, 'I left only five men with them. I'd be happier castin' my eyes over them.'

'All right,' laughed Goddard. 'Ride if you're so conscientious. Take a couple of bottles of champagne with you an' give the boys a drink. There'll be plenty back at the ranch fer riders on the other parts of the range.'

Dave Walters smiled. 'Thanks, boss,' he said enthusiastically. 'The boys'll appreciate it.'

He hurried away, collected the champagne and was soon riding out of Silverton. Walters kept his horse to a fast pace and swung across Flying F range towards the east side of the spread. Nearing the hollow he slowed the speed of his horse, not wishing to startle the men, nor the cattle by bursting over the skyline.

Dave checked his horse momentarily. He inclined his head listening for a sound he had only just missed. An anxious frown creased his forehead as he stabbed his horse forward. He felt something was wrong; cattle were never as quiet as this. Reaching the edge of the hollow he pulled on the reins with a gasp. The hollow was empty and five still forms lay around the slope! He kicked his horse into a gallop towards the nearest man. Dave was out of the saddle almost before the horse had stopped. He dropped to his knee beside the silent form, but only a casual glance was needed to tell him that the man was dead. He glanced sharply over his shoulder half expecting to see some sign of life behind him, but as he straightened himself slowly, he knew that the other four men were also dead. Anger swelled inside him, he shielded his eyes against the sun, and looked across the hollow over which there seemed to hang an air of desolation. Walters gathered up the reins of his horse and climbed wearily into the saddle. He rode slowly from man to man as a matter of duty. After examining the last body, Dave turned his attention to the tracks left by the steers. He pushed his horse to the top of the hollow, but there was no sign of the herd across the range. He stabbed his horse forward then, almost in the same moment, stopped it. Suddenly, he realised the hopelessness of the situation. The herd's tracks would be lost amongst others on the range to the south. Angrily, he pulled sharply on the reins turning his horse and kicked it into a fast, earth-pounding gallop towards Silverton.

Matt Roberts and Dan McCoy leaned against one end of the bar in the Golden Cage watching the wedding celebrations.

'This'll cost Goddard a packet,' observed Dan as the drinks flowed freely across the counter.

'He can afford it,' replied Matt wryly. 'There'll be a few drunks to see to tonight,' he added. 'They're making the most of Goddard's generosity.'

Dan studied the group which occupied the balcony at one end of the room. Bill Goddard was obviously delighted with the match, but Dan thought Pat a little on the quiet side. Stanton was beside the rail waving to some of the crowd in the saloon.

Suddenly, the batwings crashed open and Dan turned sharply to see a dust-covered Dave Walters bursting into the saloon. He paused momentarily, looking round the room. The noise subsided when the occupants saw Walters, his face grim and anxious; his chest heaving after the hard ride. Suddenly he spotted Goddard who moved nearer the rail when Pat drew his attention to his foreman. As he crossed the room Walters yelled to his boss.

'The herd's gone; our boys hev been killed!'

A gasp went round the room.

'What!' shouted Goddard, the smile disappearing from his face. He turned and hurried down the stairs, closely followed by Stanton and McLane.

Dan and Matt glanced at each other and hurried across the room to join the group which had gathered at the foot of the stairway.

'What happened, Dave?' asked Goddard anxiously.

'There was no sign of the herd when I got out there,' explained Walters, 'only five bodies – all shot.'

Goddard stared at Walters as if he couldn't believe what he heard.

'But who ... why?' he spluttered.

Walters shook his head. 'I don't know,' he whispered. 'The herd was moved south out of the hollow, but it's useless to try to pick up a trail.'

Anger swelled inside Goddard. 'Cattle just don't disappear,' he yelled. 'They must be somewhere about, an' I mean to find them.' He caught sight of Roberts. 'Wal, sheriff, what are you goin' to do about this one?'

'I'm ridin' out there right now,' replied Matt. 'An' anyone who cares to come along

131

can do so.'

'They're my cattle,' stormed Goddard. 'You aren't leavin' me behind.'

'I'll be with you,' shouted Stanton, and turning leaped up the stairs two at a time to Pat.

Several men called out that they would ride in the posse, and Dan, noticing that McLane was one of them, smiled to himself when he thought of the conversation Matt had overheard.

Matt led the posse at a fast pace, and it was a grim bunch of men that surveyed the deathly scene in the hollow.

The sheriff detailed two men to see to the dead and then led the rest of the posse southwards, but soon the tracks of the cattle were lost amongst others which marked the Flying F range.

They had been riding for half-an-hour before Matt called a halt. He leaned forward in the saddle, pushed his sombrero to the back of his head, and looked grimly at Goddard.

'Walters was right,' he said. 'It's useless to try to follow any tracks.'

'Wal, what do you propose to do about it? You're the law around here,' snapped Goddard, annoyed by the fact that he knew the sheriff was right.

'I figure we'd better return to town,' replied the sheriff coolly.

'Town!' stormed Goddard. 'You won't find my cattle there!'

'It's no good all of us stormin' across the countryside,' explained Roberts. 'Leave this to Dan and I, we'll do some scoutin'.'

'The sheriff's right, Goddard,' put in McLane. 'When he finds the rustlers we'll ride with him to…'

'McLane!' Anger flared in Goddard's eyes. 'There's been strangers around the Walking A an' thet herd wasn't far away.'

McLane stiffened. 'What you getting' at?' he hissed.

'Those men could hev operated very easily from the Walking A,' replied Goddard coolly, 'an' you could hev been behind it.'

Stanton saw that McLane was fighting hard to keep his temper, and thought it wise to step in before McLane said something which might give them away.

'McLane's all right,' he smiled. 'He couldn't hev hed anythin' to do with the rustlin', he was at the weddin', an' Clem's too thorough a man to let anyone do his rustlin' if he wanted to rustle. The sheriff's idea's a good one. Besides,' he added with a laugh, 'I want to get to my bride.'

A smile broke across Goddard's face. 'Sorry, Russ,' he said. 'You get off to Pat.' He turned to McLane.' Sorry, Clem. It was jest those strangers.'

'They were friends of mine from the old days,' he said smoothly. 'They've ridden north again.'

Goddard nodded. 'Wal, sheriff, I guess we leave things to you,' he said easily. His lips tightened. 'But I want results quick, or I handle things myself.'

# Chapter Twelve

'Wal,' drawled Matt, as they watched the posse ride away, 'where do we go from here? If Goddard cuts loose an' finds Stanton an' McLane at the bottom of this, there'll be hell let loose.'

'Let's try the hollow again,' suggested Dan. 'See if we can pick anythin' up there.'

Roberts nodded, and the two men kicked their horses forward into a trot. They kept up an easy pace, and reached the hollow to find that the two men left behind had completed their grim task, and had already left.

'We'll work opposite ways round the rim an' see if we can pick up the rustlers' tracks into the hollow,' suggested the sheriff.

Dan nodded, and the two men turned their horses and moved steadily round the hollow searching for any sign of the rustlers. Dan had ridden about four hundred yards when he pulled his horse to a halt and slipped quickly from the saddle. He dropped to his knee, and examined the ground carefully. Suddenly, he jumped to his feet, yelling

135

loudly and waving his sombrero to attract Matt's attention. As soon as the sheriff saw him, he kicked his horse into a gallop and was soon pulling up beside Dan. The young man pointed to the tracks.

'Been a few of them around here,' he said. 'Figure they came from thet direction,' he added, pointing away from the hollow.

The two men walked their horses slowly, following the tracks which led them to the spur of the hill behind the Walking A. The tracks turned down the hillside, but the two sheriffs did not go any further.

'Wal,' drawled Matt, 'seems they did come from here an' I reckon it could be no one but those strangers.'

Dan nodded. 'An' Stanton's behind the whole thing, so I guess we take a look on Stanton's range. If we want to prove anythin' we've jest got to find those cattle there.'

'We'd better fix ourselves up fer at least three days' ridin',' pointed out Matt, and the two men set their horses into a fast trot towards Silverton.

For three days the lawmen scoured Stanton's range, but could find no trace of the missing steers. It was early evening when the two weary dust-covered men rode into Silverton, thankful to be back in town. They

136

turned the tired horses into the livery stables, and walked down the main street to the hotel where they ordered a hot bath. Refreshed, they made their way to Anne's Cafe, eagerly anticipating her appetising cooking.

Anne's eyes brightened when she saw the two men walk in.

'Anythin' been happenin' around here?' asked Matt, after greetings had passed between them.

Anne smiled and shook her head. 'No,' she said. 'We don't need a sheriff in this town.' She pushed two cups of coffee to them. 'I'll soon have a meal ready for you.'

The two hungry men enjoyed their meal, and it was not until they had finished that they started to discuss the problems which faced them.

'Wonder if McLane would talk if we confronted him with our information,' said Dan, pushing his empty plate away from him.

'Don't suppose he'd believe us,' replied Matt, 'but it could be worth a try.'

'It would put a doubt in this mind an' make him think; a jealous man could stir up trouble,' pointed out Dan.

Matt nodded. 'We can ride…'

He cut his words short as the sound of a

hard ridden horse pounded in Main Street. He glanced sharply at Dan. 'I'd say this hombre was ridin' as if trouble was chasin' him.'

The two men pushed themselves away from the table and hurried across the room. Light spilled from the cafe as they opened the door and moved on to the sidewalk.

The horse thundered down the street, its hoofs pounding the hard road through the thin covering of dust. Suddenly, the rider hauled hard on the reins as he caught sight of the two men in the pool of light thrown by the kerosene lamp hanging above the doorway of Anne's Cafe. The animal tossed its head, tugging at the leather as it slid in a dust stirring halt in front of the two men.

'Roberts!' yelled the rider, surprise and anger clouding his face at the sight of the sheriff. 'Where the hell've you been?'

Annoyance flared in Matt's face. 'You know where I've been, Goddard,' he stormed. 'Tryin' to find your cattle.'

'You've been lookin' in the wrong place,' snarled the rancher. 'I've jest lost another herd!'

'What!' Matt gasped, and looked sharply at Dan who looked equally surprised.

'Yeah, at this rate I'll soon be washed out,'

138

snapped Goddard. 'An' you lawmen can do nothin' about it, so I'm takin' the law into my own hands.'

The rancher started to pull his horse round, but the sheriff stepped down quickly from the sidewalk, grasped the stirrup, and stopped his movement.

'Hold it,' snapped Matt. 'I can understand you bein' riled up...'

'Riled up!' Goddard interrupted with a laugh. 'Thet's puttin' it mildly. I'm fightin' mad, an' I'll string those rustlers up when I catch up with them.'

'Careful Goddard,' rapped Matt. 'Don't overstep the law, an' as sheriff around here, I want to know what happened.'

'The herd was jumped at dusk,' replied Goddard irritatedly. 'Took my riders by surprise, killed four of them, wounded other four an' hed the herd on the move before they knew what hed hit them.'

'Anyone get a look at the rustlers?' asked Dan.

'Nope,' Goddard shook his head. 'Their neckerchiefs were tied over their faces.'

'How many of them?' questioned Matt.

'Eight,' replied the rancher. 'I got out there as soon as I heard, but it was too dark to pick up anythin' then. Guess thet's why they hit us at dusk. They won't be able to move far in the dark, so I figured on diggin' my men out of the Golden Cage, campin' out on the range, an' hittin' the trail before sun up.'

'Right, Goddard, we'll ride with you,' said Matt. 'See you out at the Flying F.'

The rancher nodded, and kicked his horse forward towards the Golden Cage. The two lawmen watched him without speaking. He swung from the saddle and hurried across the boards to push the batwings roughly aside. A few moments later, ten men emerged from the saloon. Silently, they swung into the saddles, pulled their horses round, and rode grimly out of Silverton.

'Git two more horses, Dan,' said Matt as the last rider disappeared into the darkness. 'I'll git Anne to fix us up with some food.'

Dan hurried along the sidewalk to the livery stable and was soon back with two fresh horses. He tied them to the rail and joined Matt inside the cafe. A few minutes later, the two lawmen headed out of Silverton in the direction of the Flying F.

Goddard and his riders were mounting their horses when Matt and Dan arrived at the ranch, and as the rancher rode towards the range, the two lawmen moved alongside him.

It was a grim, determined bunch of riders that made camp for the night close to the place from which the cattle had been rustled.

Goddard had the posse awake before sun up and the eastern horizon was only just beginning to pale when they broke camp.

'They headed south,' called Goddard as Dan and Matt swung into their saddles beside him. 'I reckon they couldn't go far last night, an' we'll be pretty close to them by daylight – at least, we should be able to see their dust cloud.' Seeing all the men were mounted, the rancher pushed his horse forward into a steady gallop, and the earth shook to the pound of hoofs, as the riders closed in behind him.

Goddard watched the eastern sky brighten, feeling that with its lightness would come the sight of his missing cattle. The sun pushed an ever-increasing arc above the horizon and soon the Texas countryside was covered in its light and warmth. Goddard called a halt, and drawing a spyglass from its leather, stood in his stirrups and meticulously searched the landscape. As he finished, he slumped back into the saddle, a puzzled and disappointed man.

'Not a sign,' he muttered wearily, half to himself.

'Maybe we haven't ridden far enough,' suggested Dan, although he felt that any further attempt to discover a trail would be useless.

'Could be,' agreed Goddard, and kicked his horse forward.

The posse rode all that morning and well into the afternoon without finding a single sign of the missing herd.

'Reckon it's hopeless,' said Goddard dejectedly, as he pulled his horse to a halt, and his riders gathered round.

Loyal to their boss, the men suggested riding on, but Goddard shook his head. 'If we'd been near them, we'd hev seen some sign. We're jest wastin' our time. What do you figure, sheriff?'

'Guess you're right,' agreed Matt. 'Reckon it would be wiser to git back an' double the men with your other herds.'

The rancher laughed sarcastically. 'If I've enough men to do thet, an' if I've enough money to keep them workin' fer me. Roberts, this has hit me pretty hard an' I don't mind tellin' you it's put me into an awkward position financially.' Before anyone could comment, Goddard pulled his horse round, and put it into a steady lope across the grassland.

It was a weary party which rode into the Flying F late that evening. Goddard swung slowly from the saddle and handed the reins to one of his men. He walked wearily on to the veranda, turned and looked hard at the sheriff. Matt waited for him to speak, but, suddenly, he swung on his heels and went into the house. Dan and Matt pulled their horses round, knowing the rancher's thoughts behind that look.

'If Goddard gets an inkling of the truth, we'll hev a full scale range war on our hands,' said Roberts as they headed towards Silverton. 'The time has come to try to force the play.'

# Chapter Thirteen

Clem McLane, a look of smug self-satisfaction on his face watched the steers pour over the high narrow pass in the hills, and move down into the small secluded valley. He leaned against the doorpost of the small hut, took a long draw at his cheroot, and blew a cloud of smoke into the air with a sigh of contentment. He had done well to play along with Stanton. With this herd pouring into the valley to join the one already there, Goddard must have been dealt a crippling blow.

'Goddard must sell out now,' he whispered to himself. 'He must. Stanton an' I will own the lot.' A grin crossed his lips. 'An' Shirley will be mine.'

He watched the cowboys handle the cattle skilfully, guiding them down the hillside.

'Butch sure knows his job,' he muttered. 'Couldn't hev hed a better man fer this set up.' His tone had a touch of self-praise about it, remembering that it was he who had brought in Butch and his gang from Missouri.

The riders drove the cattle along the short valley until the two herds were mingling together. It wasn't until he was satisfied that the steers were settling down that Butch called his men away. Relief crossed their faces, they relaxed in the saddles, turned their horses, and galloped towards the hut.

Butch reined his horse to a halt in front of McLane. He pulled the neckerchief off the lower half of his face, and grinned at McLane as he wiped the dust and sweat from his face.

'Sure went smooth,' he said, swinging from the saddle. 'No trouble at all.'

McLane smiled contentedly. 'Nice work, Butch.' He turned to the others who were slapping dust from their clothes. 'There's a drink inside,' he called, and turned into the hut, followed by the eight men. 'Anyone follow you?' he asked.

'Nope,' replied Butch, pouring himself a drink. 'Thanks to Charlie's knowledge of the land we were able to keep moving all night, an' were well up towards the pass by daybreak.'

'Good,' said McLane. 'I figure Stanton will be mighty pleased when I git back an' tell him all has gone well.'

'What's our next move?' asked Butch.

'Relax until you hear from me or Stanton,' replied Clem. 'Keep someone up at the pass,' he suggested. 'Don't suppose anyone will trouble you out here, but it's best to be on the safe side.'

'How come Goddard doesn't know about this place?' asked Butch curiously. 'It's his land isn't it?'

McLane nodded. 'Sure is, but don't forgit these hills are pretty barren,' he pointed out. 'They're right on the edge of his territory, so I guess he hasn't bothered explorin' them. There's no sign of this valley from the other side of the hills. You wouldn't know anythin' about the pass unless you rode on to it accidentally, same as Stanton did.'

Butch nodded. 'Figures,' he said, and finished his drink.

McLane picked up his Stetson, and made towards the door, followed by Butch. 'Wal, I guess I can ride now,' he said. 'Stanton will be anxious to know what happened.'

He untied his horse from the rail, climbed into the saddle, and with a brief wave to Butch, sent his horse at a steady trot towards the hills. His pace slowed as he started to climb, and when he reached the pass, he paused, looking back into the valley of lush grass enclosed by steep-sided hills,

146

realising that indirectly his fortune and future lay there.

McLane rode steadily; he had a long ride ahead of him, and, although he was eager to reach the Broken C, he knew that Stanton could not approach Goddard with his proposition immediately. About three o'clock in the afternoon McLane suddenly stiffened in the saddle. He pulled his horse to a halt, and shielding his eyes from the glare of the sun stared across the grassland. The heat sent a shimmering haze across his vision and at first McLane thought his eyes deceived him. He waited patiently for a few minutes, staring into the distance until he was certain that he was not mistaken. Several figures moved slowly across the grassland!

He glanced anxiously around, and seeing a slight rise about a quarter of a mile to his right, sent his horse towards it, careful not to raise any dust. He slipped from the saddle, left his horse at the bottom of the slope, and crept to the top. The riders moved slowly, stopping every now and again. McLane watched carefully for about half an hour.

'Searchin',' he muttered to himself. 'Must be a posse.'

The rancher from Roaring Valley, deciding that his best policy was to stay where he was, settled down to wait. Slowly the riders drew nearer; it seemed like eternity before McLane could pick out their number. All the time they appeared to be searching the ground, and the watching man was thankful that they had not picked up a trail. Should they do so, McLane realised he would have to change his plans quickly. As they moved through the grasslands, McLane began to get anxious, wondering if they had planned to spend the night on the range and resume their search in the morning, but his fears were dispelled when, about six o'clock, he saw the posse halt for a few minutes, then suddenly turn their horses and send them into a gallop in the direction from which they had come.

McLane breathed a sigh of relief as he watched the dust cloud move away. He slipped quickly down the hillside, swung into the saddle, and kicked his horse into a gallop. It had been his intention to return to the Walking A before riding to see Stanton, but after the delay, Clem kept to a trail which took him above the head of Roaring Valley and on to Broken C land.

Darkness was closing in on the Texas countryside and lights shone from the ranch-house as Clem galloped up to the Broken C.

He was out of the saddle quickly and was soon shown into a room where Russ Stanton and Pat were just starting a meal.

Surprise showed on Stanton's face when he saw the dust-covered man. Pat glanced curiously at him, but quickly turned her attention back to the table.

'Hello, Clem, looks as if you've had some hard ridin',' greeted Stanton indicating the travel-stained clothes.

'Sure hev,' replied McLane who, with a slight inclination of his head, indicated that he wanted to see Stanton alone. 'I hope you'll excuse my appearance, Pat.'

Pat acknowledged his apology with a faint smile.

'I guess you'll be ready fer a meal,' said Russ, pushing himself from the table. 'Pat,' he went on, turning to his wife, 'Clem an' I hev somethin' to talk over; get Joey to set another place; Clem will join us in a few moments.'

Pat nodded without saying a word, and the two men left the room, crossed the hall, and entered Stanton's study.

'Where the hell hev you been?' snapped Stanton as the door closed behind him.

'Got held up,' replied McLane. Stanton looked concerned and McLane hastened to

149

add 'No, Russ, everythin' is all right. The herd came in as planned; Butch hed no trouble at all.'

'Good.' Relief showed in Stanton's voice. He crossed to a heavy oak sideboard, and took out two glasses and a bottle of whisky. 'Then why hev you been so long?' he asked, as he poured out the drinks.

McLane told his story, enjoying his whisky as he did so.

'Good work, Clem,' grinned Stanton when Clem had finished. 'I'm glad you stayed to keep that posse under observation, if they'd got on to the trail of those steers we'd hev hed to think again. Goddard must be hit pretty hard.' He slapped McLane on the back. 'Get cleaned up, then join Pat an' I. You can really enjoy this meal, knowin' we'll soon hev the Flying F. I'll ride over there tomorrow an' see what Goddard has to say, may be he'll be ready to sell out.'

McLane grinned. 'Then you an' I'll rule this countryside an' Silverton will be in our pockets.'

Stanton smiled to himself as he thought of what he had in store for McLane when the time came, but his voice did not betray his thoughts when he spoke. 'Sure, we'll control the lot before we're through!'

Pat awoke the following morning to find the sunlight streaming through the window. Realising that she had overslept, she jumped out of bed quickly, slipped her feet into a pair of slippers, and pulled her dressing gown around her as she crossed to the window. She was startled when she saw a cowboy leading her horse, already saddled, along with her husband's, towards the house. Pat, a frown puckering her brow, and her lips pursed thoughtfully, turned slowly from the window. She had not ordered her horse for a morning ride, so why was it being brought to the house?

Her thoughts were interrupted as the door of the bedroom opened, and her husband walked in.

'Ah, you're awake,' he said with a smile. 'I let you sleep on until Joey had breakfast almost ready.'

Pat looked curiously at Stanton. 'Why the horses?' she asked.

'Oh, you've seen them,' he replied. 'Wal, I hev to make a call this morning, and I knew you'd want to come with me so the...'

'What's wrong?' interrupted Pat sharply, sensing that her husband was leading up to something.

'Clem brought some bad news,' answered

Stanton. 'Your father's had another herd rustled!'

'What!' gasped Pat. 'Why didn't you tell me last night?' Anger flashed in her eyes. 'We should have gone to him straight away.'

'We couldn't have done any good last night,' pointed out Stanton, as Pat paced the room. 'I didn't want to alarm you, I thought it better for you to have a good night's sleep before you heard the news.'

'That was nice of you,' said Pat sarcastically as she spun round to face Stanton. 'Now get out, and let me get ready,' she snapped angrily. 'I'll be down in a moment.'

Stanton left the room without a further word, and a few minutes later when Pat, dressed ready for riding, came into the dining room, he was already having his breakfast. The news had driven all thought of food from Pat's mind, but she gulped down a cup of coffee, and urged her husband to hurry. Soon they were riding away from the Broken C at a fast gallop.

The sound of hard-ridden horses brought Bill Goddard on to the veranda of his ranch-house. His eyes narrowed against the sun as he stared to see who approached the Flying F.

'Pat,' he muttered to himself. At the sight

of his daughter the tension went out of his body and as he leaned heavily on the rail, it eased his worried mind to admire the way in which Pat handled her horse.

Pat swung out of the saddle as she pulled to a halt in front of the house. Leaping up the steps she kissed her father, hugging him tightly.

'You all right, Dad?' asked Pat anxiously.

Goddard nodded.

'Russ only told me this morning,' went on Pat breathlessly. 'We came straight away.'

'Clem McLane brought the news last night,' explained Stanton, striding on to the veranda, after hitching the horses to the rail. 'But I thought it best not to worry Pat until this morning.'

'Quite right,' agreed Goddard, leading the way into the house.

'What happened?' asked Stanton, as they entered the room.

'The herd was jumped at sundown,' explained the rancher. A lot of my boys were in town an' by the time I'd gathered them into a posse, it was too late to do anythin'. I figured we'd catch up with them yesterday mornin' but no luck; they must hev driven all night.'

'Then it must be someone who knows the

country,' pointed out Pat.

Goddard stroked his chin thoughtfully. 'Thet figures,' he said. 'But who?'

'Any of your boys recognise any of them?' asked Stanton.

Goddard shook his head. 'They were all masked this time, but I figure it must be the same bunch as jumped the first herd.'

'How many lost this time, Dad?' asked Pat.

'Five hundred an' with the first thousand, you'll know I've been pretty hard hit,' replied her father downheartedly. 'Most of thet bunch were goin' up to Missouri next month. Can't see how I can re-stock without thet sale. I've jest got to find those steers,' he added desperately.

'But won't the bank loan you something if necessary?' asked Pat.

Goddard smiled wryly. ''Fraid no,' he replied. 'You see I'm overdrawn already.' Seeing Pat's eyes widen with surprise, her father went on. 'I gambled on buying more land to the west and increasing my herds, and I'm afraid I borrowed a large sum to do that.' He shook his head. 'I can't see the bank loanin' me any more.'

Pat looked desperately at Stanton. 'Russ, you can lend Dad what he wants,' she urged.

Stanton smiled faintly, and shook his head. 'Wish I could,' he lied, 'but I'm in the red with the bank as well. Only just, mind you, an' I dare say I could borrow some more but if I tried they'd want to know all about it an' they'd want a good security. I'm afraid your father isn't that at the moment.'

Pat, her face clouded with worry, stared anxiously at the two men. 'What are we going to do?' she asked.

'Wal,' replied her father. 'I'm goin' to do some more scoutin', see if I can't git on the trail of those steers.'

'Of course, there's one way out of this,' drawled Stanton thoughtfully.

Pat's eyes brightened. 'Well, what is it?' she asked eagerly, as her husband hesitated.

'I reckon the bank would loan me the cash to buy the Flying F, there'd always be the ranch as surety,' he explained.

'What? Sell the Flying F,' gasped Pat, startled by the suggestion. 'But...'

'Never!' cried Goddard, taken aback by the thought of losing the ranch he had patiently built up over the years. 'I'll do anythin' rather than thet!'

'It was only an idea,' replied Stanton. 'I thought this was an easy way out of your difficulties.'

Goddard crossed the room to the door. 'It was a thought,' he said, 'but I'm ridin' south first.' Suddenly, he swung round and for a moment stared thoughtfully at Stanton.

'You said it was McLane who told you about the rustlin'?' he rapped.

Stanton nodded.

'Wonder how he knew?' he mused.

Stanton shrugged his shoulders. 'Don't know,' he replied. 'But news has a habit of travellin' fast.'

Goddard stroked his chin. 'Strange thet the rustlin' should happen after several strangers hev been around the Walkin' A.'

'But McLane explained thet,' pointed out Stanton.

'I'm not so sure,' answered Goddard. 'I reckon thet hombre's worth a visit. Come on I'll ride thet way with you before headin' south.'

Little was said on the ride to the Walking A, and as they approached the ranch-house Russ Stanton was more than anxious in case his hand was suddenly forced when Goddard faced McLane. He was relieved when they found McLane was not at home.

'Wal, I guess I can call when I get back,' said Goddard, somewhat annoyed that his journey had been fruitless.

156

'Take care, Dad,' cautioned Pat, bidding him goodbye. As she watched him ride towards the hillside, anxiety filled her mind.

'Guess we may as well git back home,' rapped Stanton, breaking into her thoughts. 'If he won't sell out to me, I don't see how I can help him.'

Pat did not reply and hardly spoke as they crossed Roaring Valley. She looked curiously at her husband as they climbed towards Broken C range.

'What did McLane want to see you about last night?' she asked suddenly.

Stanton, taken aback by the suddenness of the question, glanced sharply at his wife. 'Nothin' really,' he stammered. 'Only something to do with the water rights in Roaring Valley,' he added quickly.

'Seems strange that he should brings news of the rustlin'; he'd done a lot of riding by his appearance; could be he knows something about it,' she said thoughtfully. She watched her husband carefully, but he did not reply. 'It was strange how he should get the Walking A after John Denston's killing. Everything could fit together.'

The horses topped the slope, and Stanton pulled to a halt. He eased himself in the saddle, and turned to his wife.

'What you gettin' at?' he asked icily.

'Funny that Dad's cattle should be rustled,' went on Pat quietly, disregarding her husband's question. 'McLane hasn't lost any … nor have you!'

Stanton eyed his wife coldly. 'You're havin' foolish ideas,' he said. 'They're better left alone!'

Stanton pulled his horse round sharply, and stabbed it into a gallop in the direction of the ranch. Pat, feeling that she had startled Stanton, grinned to herself and kicked her horse into a gallop to catch up with her husband.

'In a mighty hurry all of a sudden,' called Pat, as they pulled up outside the ranch-house.

'Got somethin' thet needs attendin' to,' replied Stanton as he dropped out of the saddle and hurried towards the bunkhouse, outside of which he had seen Jed Roscoe's horse.

He swung open the door, and hurried inside. 'Everythin' in order, Jed?' he asked, as the foreman turned to see who had entered the room.

'Sure, boss,' replied Roscoe. 'I've jest come back from checkin' the herds.'

'Good, I've a job fer you.' Stanton issued his orders quickly. 'Git over to the Flying F an' tell Shorty to trail Goddard. He's headin' south, hopin' to find his cattle. Then you git back to the Walkin' A an' keep your eye on McLane. Goddard's suspicious of him, an' may visit him when he gits back. I'll send Curley to Butch an' tell him to hit Goddard again tonight.' His eyes narrowed, and his lips tightened. 'I'll make that hombre crawl back to me,' he spat, viciously.

'Things warmin' up, boss?' grinned Roscoe. 'Do I ... if necessary?' he patted his holster.

Stanton nodded, and the two men hurried from the room.

Pat, who had lingered on the veranda of the house, stiffened when she saw the two men emerge. A worried frown creased her forehead, and she bit her lip as she watched Roscoe swing into the saddle, and stir the dust as he left the Broken C at a fast gallop.

## Chapter Fourteen

Dan McCoy and Matt Roberts left Silverton at a steady trot and headed in the direction of the Flying F.

'I reckon your idea to put Goddard into the picture before we tackle McLane is a good one,' called Matt as he pulled his horse closer to the young sheriff from Red Springs.

'Probably won't believe us,' answered Dan.

'No, but it may stop him from taking things too much into his own hands, and give us time to test McLane,' pointed out Matt.

Dan nodded. 'We've jest got to force this affair now.'

When they reached the Flying F, the two lawmen were greeted by the foreman, Dave Walters.

'Boss around?' asked Matt.

'Nope,' replied Walters.

Matt looked sharply at Dan, wondering if they were too late.

'Any idea where he went?' queried the sheriff.

'Nope,' answered the foreman tersely. 'Rode out of here with his daughter an' Stanton if thet means anythin' to you.'

Dan felt the relief in the sheriff's voice as he thanked Walters. 'Guess we visit McLane now,' he added, turning to Dan.

It was not long before the two men were pulling up outside the Walking A, only to find that McLane was also away from home.

'Any idea where he is?' asked the sheriff of the cowboy who appeared on their arrival.

The man shook his head.

'Guess we'll stick around 'til he gits back,' said Matt, slipping from the saddle.

The man grunted and started to walk towards the bunkhouse.

'Charlie around?' asked Dan sharply.

The cowboy stopped and turned slowly, eyeing the lawmen curiously. 'You're mighty interested in men thet aren't here,' he drawled. 'Charlie's been gone a few days.'

Dan looked thoughtfully at Matt, who met his glance. 'Reckon Charlie's with the gang,' said Dan as he sat down beside Matt on the veranda. 'They couldn't hev moved thet herd all night without local knowledge an' Charlie's supplyin' it.'

'It all fits,' agreed Matt, 'but I guess we'll hev to be patient until McLane gits back.'

The two men settled down to wait, little knowing that at that moment Clem McLane was strolling into the Golden Cage.

There were only four cowboys in the saloon when the rancher from Roaring Valley pushed aside the batwings, whistling happily to himself. He had taken some care over his dress that morning, and was immaculately turned out, and had even dispensed with his gunbelt. He felt this was his day, and a Colt would not be necessary for the important event he was to precipitate in a few minutes.

'Mornin',' Clem greeted the barman cheerily. 'Shirley in her room?'

'Yes,' came the reply.

McLane climbed the stairs and hurried along the balcony to tap lightly on the door at the end nearest the stage.

'Come in,' called Shirley pleasantly.

'Good mornin', sweetheart,' greeted McLane as he closed the door behind him.

The girl looked a little startled when she saw McLane. 'You're an early visitor, Clem,' she said. 'What brings you to town at this time of day?'

McLane hurried across the room.

'You,' he said, encircling her waist with his arms, and pulling her towards him.

162

She stiffened, her hands pressing against his chest, trying to push him off, but he bent forward eagerly to kiss her. Shirley pressed herself backwards, turning her lips away from his, her face showing a dislike of the attentions being shown towards her. McLane looked surprised, and as his grip around her waist relaxed, the singer twisted away from him.

'What's the matter?' asked McLane, astonished by Shirley's reactions. 'You've never been like this before.'

Shirley looked down, straightening her dress. 'Nothin',' she answered quietly, 'but you don't generally call at this time of day.'

McLane looked a little relieved. 'This is a special day,' he said eagerly.

'Why?' asked Shirley, eyeing him curiously.

Clem stepped forward. 'First a kiss,' he said, encircling her waist once more.

Shirley stiffened again, but kissed him lightly without any feeling. Anger, mingled with surprise, crossed McLane's face as he released her.

'Somethin's wrong, Shirley, what is it?' he snapped.

'Nothing, Clem, nothing,' answered the girl. 'I'm not feeling too well,' she lied.

'If thet's all it is,' said McLane, 'then maybe my askin' you to marry me will fix things up.'

Shirley gasped and stared at McLane. Suddenly, she burst out laughing. McLane, unable to understand her outburst stood and stared.

'You do look funny, Clem,' laughed Shirley, 'looking angry and surprised at my rebuffs, and, at the same time, proposing to me.'

McLane stepped forward, annoyance crossing his face. 'I'm serious, Shirley, this is no laughing matter.' He grasped her firmly by the shoulders, his grip tightening as she continued to laugh.

Suddenly she stopped, and winced with pain. 'You're hurting me, Clem,' she gasped as the man's fingers dug into her shoulders.

McLane did not release his grip. He looked deep into the girl's eyes. 'I asked you a question, and it wants an answer,' he hissed sharply. The girl did not reply, and Clem continued eagerly. 'Things are breaking our way. Stanton will soon force Goddard to sell the Flying F an' part of it will be mine – no, ours; with you as my wife, you'll share it.'

Shirley pushed Clem away, shuddering as his hands slid from her body. Her eyes widened, flashing scornfully.

'Fool!' she mocked. Her lips curled with contempt. 'You're content to take the pickings of other men's brains. Do you think Russ would let you have one small part of it, when he planned everything?' Her voice rose shrilly. 'You are only a tool to be thrown away when no longer required!' Shirley paused, gasping for breath.

McLane stared incredulously at her. He gasped, unable to believe the words she hurled at him.

'You think I'd want to marry you,' the girl continued scathingly, 'the underdog; the little man who tries to look big; the pawn for a man like Stanton.'

McLane's brain pounded as the words burst in his ears.

'I don't want you,' screamed Shirley. 'Only the top man's good enough for me!'

'But he's married already,' McLane protested weakly.

'Maybe,' lashed back the girl, 'but Pat is going the same way as her father; the same way as you are going.' Her eyes flashed with triumph. 'Then Russ and I will rule the lot.'

She drew herself up, staring mockingly at Clem who was badly shaken by all that he had heard. He spluttered, trying to speak, but Shirley's voice still pounded his brain so that he was unable to find his words. He stumbled slowly towards her, but she stood her ground.

'Get out!' she screamed. 'Get out!'

McLane was upon her, his eyes wild with anger. He grasped her tight round the neck, forcing her back on to the sofa.

'Clem!' she cried, but the word was choked into a gurgle as his grip tightened upon her throat. Her eyes widened with terror as McLane leaned over her, forcing her harder into the sofa. Her hands grasped his wrists, struggling in vain to break their grip. Slowly the life was being driven from her body.

Suddenly, McLane's grip relaxed. He pulled himself upright, panting hard as Shirley's hands flew to her neck, rubbing it tenderly whilst she gasped for breath, watching McLane with frightened eyes. Suddenly, the rancher leaned forward and slashed her hard across her face with the back of his hand, jerking her head sideways. She cried out with the pain, and tears flowed from her eyes.

'Killin' you would be too good,' snarled Clem. 'You'll be mine yet, an' you'll want me because I'll be top dog after I've dealt with your precious Russ Stanton!'

McLane turned on his heel, and stormed

from the room, slamming the door behind him. He strode angrily along the balcony, into the saloon, and without looking at the men at the bar, slammed out through the batwings. He jerked the reins from the rail, swung quickly into the saddle, and left the main street of Silverton in a dust stirring gallop.

He headed east, away from the town, his brain still pounding with the news he had just heard. McLane had ridden two miles before his mind began to think reasonably again, and began to get a grip on himself, to think things out carefully. As he eased himself in the saddle, turning over in his mind his approach to Stanton, his right hand moved to feel his holster reassuringly. Suddenly, he started and jerked hard on the reins to bring the horse slithering in the dust to a halt. He had no gun-belt! The dust swirled round man and animal. McLane cursed loudly, pulled his horse round sharply, and put it into a fast gallop towards the Walking A.

Shirley did not move as Clem McLane slammed the door. She lay with her head buried in the cushions on the sofa, her body shaken by her sobbing, as tears flowed. A jarring pain tore at her face where McLane had struck her, and an ugly redness marked her cheek. Five minutes passed before the full meaning of McLane's threat struck into her numb brain.

She shoved herself from the sofa and, wiping her eyes, she hurried into her dressing room, where she changed quickly into her riding outfit of tight black jeans, green blouse, and black riding-boots. Shirley realised that she must reach Stanton quickly, but already McLane had had a good start on her. She ran from the room, tying a neckerchief at her throat as she did so. The few occupants of the bar stared as she half walked, and half ran along the balcony, down the stairs, and crossed the saloon without a glance at anyone.

The singer ran across the street to the livery stables, and told the stable-boy to hurry with her horse. She paced up and down impatiently as he prepared the animal for the ride. He had hardly finished adjusting the stirrups before she grabbed the reins, swung on to the horse's back, and sent it at a fast gallop along the eastern road, out of Silverton. Impatiently, she urged the animal faster and faster, and in answer to her call it stretched itself in an earth pounding gallop across the Texas countryside. Time seemed to stand still to the girl as the wind whistled past her ears, and she remembered little of the ride, except the wave of relief which seemed to flood her body when the Broken C buildings came in sight, and a rider whom she recognised as Russ Stanton came galloping towards her.

Her brain pounded; she was in time; how she had beaten McLane she did not know, but, somehow, she had reached Russ before him and to her that was all that mattered.

Stanton slowed his horse as they neared each other, but Shirley Parker did not ease her gallop until she was almost upon the rancher. Pulling hard on the reins, she dragged the animal to a sliding dust-raising halt, close to Stanton.

'Shirley, what's the matter?' he shouted, leaning forward and grabbing the reins to steady her horse.

Relief showed in the girl's face as she relaxed in the saddle. 'I'm glad to see you,' she panted. 'I thought I wouldn't be in time.' She paused, her chest heaving as she gulped air into her aching lungs.

'In time?' puzzled Stanton. 'At thet speed you'd be in time fer anythin'. Saw your dust cloud, an' wondered who was in a mighty rush. My spyglass showed me it was you, so thought I'd better ride to meet you as Pat is at home.'

'Russ, I'm sorry,' panted Shirley, 'but I've spilled everything to Clem.'

'What!' gasped Stanton, anger showing momentarily in his face.

'He came to see me this morning,' explained Shirley, 'and when he proposed the way he did, pawing over me, I just couldn't stand it any longer.' She paused, searching Stanton's face for understanding, but the rancher remained impassive, and did not speak. 'He almost murdered me, Russ,' went on Shirley. 'Then he left me, saying he would get you instead. I came straight out here to warn you.' She slumped in the saddle, her strength sapped by the shock of her encounter with McLane, and the tension of the hard, exhausting ride.

Stanton leaned forward, putting his arm round her, and supporting her whilst he put his hip flask of brandy to her lips. The girl shuddered, as the spirit drove into her body. She straightened herself in the saddle, and shook her hair back from her face, which she wiped with the neckerchief offered by Stanton.

The first annoyance at the news had disappeared from Stanton's face. 'Stop worryin', Shirley,' he smiled. 'McLane hasn't been this way yet, and now, thanks to you, I'm forewarned, so our clever Mister McLane can expect an unpleasant reception.'

'I can't understand why he didn't get here before me,' said Shirley.

'Maybe he's changed his mind,' grinned Stanton. 'Or jest gone back to the Walking A first. If he's done thet, he'll be watched; Jed Roscoe's over there to keep an eye on him.'

Shirley looked surprised. 'Why?' she asked.

'Goddard suspects McLane's behind the rustlings,' explained Russ, 'an' he said he would tackle McLane. If Goddard gets rough, Clem might talk, so Roscoe an' his rifle are keepin' their sights on McLane.' The rancher paused, eased his horse close to the girl's, and leaning towards her, kissed her lightly. 'Now, you get back to town, and don't worry any more; you'll soon be mine.'

Shirley smiled, and returned his kiss, before pulling her horse round and sending it at an easy pace towards Silverton.

Matt Roberts and Dan McCoy sat on the steps of the veranda of the Walking A, watching the cowhand walk to the bunkhouse. As the door closed behind him Dan turned to Matt.

'Look here,' he said, 'there is a possibility thet the deeds to this property may still be here.'

'But they were stolen the night John Denston was killed,' pointed out Matt.

'I know,' agreed Dan, 'but if McLane's deep in this, then they may have been brought back here.'

'Possibly,' said Matt, 'but if...'

'Then let's take a look round whilst we're here,' urged Dan.

'It's worth a try,' consented the Sheriff of Silverton.

The two men clambered to their feet, and finding the door of the house open went inside. They searched the rooms quickly and methodically, but found nothing which would help them prove that the Walking A and Roaring Valley were still the property of Anne Denston.

Whilst they were engrossed in their search a lone cowboy broke the skyline of the hill behind the house and rode slowly down towards the valley. Suddenly, he pulled his horse to a halt and stared for a few moments at the two horses tied to the rail in front of the ranch-house below him.

'Lawmen,' hissed Roscoe to himself, when he recognised the horses.

He slipped from the saddle, and led his horse carefully until he reached the cover of a group of boulders about a hundred yards from the house. After securing the animal, he drew his rifle from the leather scabbard. Slipping from cover to cover he reached the house quickly. Carefully he moved along the walls and peered cautiously in each window, but saw no one, until he reached the open window of McLane's main room. Relief swept over the tensed Roscoe when he saw that Clem McLane was not with the sheriffs.

He returned swiftly to the cover of the boulders, where he had been waiting about ten minutes when the sound of a hard ridden horse attracted his attention. A few moments later, he realised that the two lawmen had also heard the pound of the hoofs when they appeared on the veranda.

'Seems McLane's in a mighty hurry over something,' commented Dan, as the two men leaned on the rail and watched the occupier of the Walking A approach.

McLane pulled hard on the reins when he reached the house, bringing his sweating mount to a sliding halt. Surprise and annoyance showed on his face at the sight of the lawmen.

'What brings you here?' he snapped,

swinging from the saddle and striding past them into the house.

The two men followed him inside, and as they did so, Roscoe slipped from his hiding place, and leading his horse, moved towards the house.

'We want a word with you,' said Matt. 'We hev something of interest to tell you.'

'I've hed enough told me today,' snarled McLane. He snatched his gunbelt from a chair, and fastened it quickly round his waist. 'I jest want to git at Stanton now.' He pulled the leather thong at the tip of his holster tightly round his thigh, and tested the hang of his Colt.

Matt looked sharply at Dan. 'Hold on!' snapped the sheriff. 'You'd better curb that temper an' hear what we hev to say first.'

'All right,' snapped McLane. 'I can't give you long, so git on with it.'

Roberts quickly told McLane of the plans he had overheard Stanton making with Shirley Parker.

Before Matt finished, McLane started to laugh. 'Thet's old news now, sheriff,' he broke in. 'Shirley told me it all this morning, an' I could tell you a whole heap more thet would make you sit up an' take notice, but I haven't got time. I want to deal with Stanton myself,' he added viciously, striding towards the door.

Dan pulled his Colt from its holster. 'Hold it, McLane!' he snapped.

Clem stopped, as he recognised the warning note in Dan's voice. He turned round slowly, anger flaring in his eyes.

'Put thet back,' he snarled, indicating the gun. 'After the way Stanton's played me along, I want to deal with him now.'

'McLane!' rapped Roberts. 'You can't take the law into your own hands. Tell us all you know an' let us deal with him.'

McLane grinned, and shook his head. 'No,' he replied coldly. 'Thet would be too good fer him.'

'You won't pull it off,' said Matt hastily. 'He's faster on the draw than you.'

'He won't git a chance to draw on me,' hissed McLane, 'and I'm going to make thet dirty double-crosser crawl on his knees an' beg forgiveness before I kill him.'

Dan sensed the vicious hate in the man in front of him. 'If you kill in cold blood you'll swing,' he said quietly but firmly, making the meaning of his words felt. 'You'll lose everythin'; you still won't hev Shirley, so what's the sense in you killin' Stanton?'

'Come on, give us the whole story,' pressed

175

Roberts. 'Wouldn't thet be a better way to git even with Stanton?'

McLane looked thoughtfully at the two men, and then walked slowly across the room to a table near the open window, and poured himself a glass of whisky, which he swallowed in one gulp.

'Guess you're right,' he said as he replaced the glass on the table. His eyes narrowed, twinkling with amusement at his thoughts. 'It will turn the tables on Stanton, an' with him out of the way, I'll hev Shirley.' He indicated two chairs. 'Sit down,' he said. 'I'll tell you everythin'.'

Dan slipped his Colt back into its holster, and the two men sat down eager to hear McLane's story.

'Wal,' drawled Clem, 'it all began with Stanton wantin' Roaring Valley, then owned by John Denston. He persuaded me to...'

His words were cut short as a gun roared from the open window behind McLane. He gasped, his eyes widening with surprise. Slowly, his knees buckled, and he pitched forward on to the floor in front of the two lawmen, who were momentarily taken aback by the ear-shattering noise. As McLane fell at their feet, Matt was on his knees beside him and Dan, jerking his Colt from its

176

holster, leaped towards the window, but when he looked outside, there was only the sound of a galloping horse to mock his ears.

'See anyone?' shouted Matt.

'No,' answered Dan, as he turned and ran for the door. 'But I'll git after him.'

He ran onto the veranda, pushed his Colt into its holster, unhitched his horse, and leaped into the saddle, turning the powerful black as he did so. The animal quickly stretched itself into a gallop, and hoofs pounded the earth as it tried to close the gap between Dan and the fleeing cowboy who was heading towards the head of Roaring Valley. The distance between them closed steadily, but when the killer reached the rougher ground of the narrowing, boulder-strewn valley, the pace slackened, and Dan kept losing sight of the cowboy as he twisted between the huge boulders.

The ride became harder as they neared the waterfall which pounded the rocks in a great roar, sending a veil of spray across the head of the valley. Suddenly, Dan pulled his horse to a stop and shielded his eyes against the spray. The rider was nowhere to be seen. Through narrowed eyes, Dan searched the terrain ahead, but could see no sign of the horseman.

'Reckon he's goin' to make a stand behind those rocks,' muttered Dan. He slipped from the saddle, drew his Colt, and crept cautiously forward towards a large group of huge boulders, behind which he had last seen the man ride.

Although he used every available cover, Dan was surprised that the man did not fire at him. Reaching the group of boulders, he moved carefully round them, only to find both man and horse had disappeared.

A small, flat expanse of rock stretched in front of him, and somewhat mystified, Dan searched around for some sign of the killer, but without success.

He turned his eyes to the waterfall, searching for some path the killer might have taken, but the wall of rock on this side of the river was too steep. Only on the opposite side was a possible means of escape as Dan well remembered from his own escape from over the head of the valley a few days previously.

He moved to the edge of the rock and found himself looking into a gorge through which the water churned fifty feet below. He rubbed his chin thoughtfully, wondering if the man could have leaped the gorge, but concluded that it was too wide even for his strong muscular horse to jump.

Puzzled, Dan was turning away, when suddenly he stiffened. A black sombrero, tossed and turned by the whirling water, span round in a little pool carved out under some overhanging rock. Dan watched the hat for a moment as it tried to escape from the clutching whirlpool, knowing that it had been a chance in a thousand that had taken it there to indicate the fate of its owner. Quickly, Dan turned his attention to the dancing waters of the river, searching for some other sign of the killer, but he realised that nothing could survive in the pounding waters, and both man and animal must by now be far down the river. He holstered his Colt and turned from the edge of the rock, shuddering at the horrible fate which had awaited McLane's killer as he plunged into the gorge.

Reaching his horse he climbed into the saddle, and headed down the valley, only hurrying the black when it reached the grassland as the valley widened. When Dan pulled up outside the Walking A ranch-house he found Matt anxiously awaiting his return.

'Any luck?' he asked.

Dan shook his head and quickly told his story of the pursuit.

'Any idea who it was?' questioned Matt, when Dan finished speaking.

'Wal,' drawled Dan thoughtfully, 'it wasn't Goddard, this hombre sat a horse differently, and wasn't as big. I reckon it could hev been Roscoe, but I'm not certain.'

'No matter, if he's dead,' said Matt. 'If it was Roscoe then Stanton's been suspicious of McLane, or decided to eliminate him sooner than he indicated to Shirley Parker thet night I saw them together.' He paused thoughtfully. 'There'll be no need to tell Goddard of our suspicions now McLane's dead,' he added.

Dan nodded his agreement. 'All the same,' he said, 'I reckon it might be as well if I kept an eye on Goddard.'

# Chapter Fifteen

The two lawmen parted at the Walking A, and as Matt Roberts returned to Silverton, Dan McCoy put his horse up the hillside on to Flying F range. When the ranch buildings came into view, Dan proceeded cautiously, and keeping to the cover of some cotton-woods, found an advantageous point from which to watch the house.

The light was beginning to fade from the sky when the clop of a horse's hoofs sharp-ened Dan's attention. A few moments later the owner of the Flying F came into view. He was slumped in the saddle, his shoulders rounded; his head sunk forward; and when he climbed from the horse he looked a tired, worn-out man.

Suddenly Dan stiffened. Another horse approached from the same direction.

'Shorty Best!' muttered Dan to himself when he saw the man.

Shorty halted his horse and sat perfectly still watching the rancher, who scraped wearily across the boards and entered the house. As the door closed behind Goddard, the cowboy turned his horse and rode away from the Flying F.

Dan was puzzled by the man's behaviour, and realising that Goddard was so weary that he would only ride in an emergency, Dan hurried to his horse, swung quickly into the saddle, and rode after Shorty. He was relieved when the silhouette of the rider appeared in the gathering darkness, and Dan matched the pace of the man ahead. He kept at a steady lope into Roaring Valley, and it was not long before Dan realised that Shorty was heading for the Broken C.

As the buildings loomed ahead, Dan proceeded cautiously, and leaving his horse some distance from the house, he hurried forward on foot, and was just in time to see Shorty admitted to the house. Dan glanced anxiously around; there was no movement anywhere, and the only sign of life was the light which streamed from the windows of the bunkhouse about two hundred yards beyond the main building. The sheriff from Red Springs raced forward, and reaching the house flattened himself against the wall. He listened for a moment but all was quiet. Dan eased his Colt in its holster and crept swiftly along the side of the building to the corner, round which he peered cautiously. A dim light came from a window a few paces away, and when he reached it, he found the curtains were drawn. He could hear the mumble of voices inside the room, and recognising Stanton and Shorty, he pressed himself closer to the curtained window, to catch their words.

'Good work, Shorty,' praised Stanton. 'You're sure Goddard didn't spot you trailin' him?'

'Never caught a glimpse of me, an' he never saw any signs of the cattle,' assured the cowboy.

'Wal, I reckon you can stick around here now, Shorty,' instructed Stanton. 'Things are going to happen tomorrow, an' I reckon it won't be long before Goddard comes in thet door beggin' me to buy his ranch.'

Dan heard the clink of glasses, and the closing of a door. He reckoned he would learn no more and made his way back round the building. Suddenly, he froze when he heard the front door of the house open, and boots clatter on to the veranda.

'You'll find a spare bunk, all right, Shorty.'
'Thanks, Mister Stanton, goodnight.'
'Goodnight!'
Dan heard the door close and waited

patiently until Shorty's footsteps faded towards the bunkhouse, and the door closed behind him.

He ran swiftly to his horse, swung into the saddle, and sent the animal at a fast pace towards Silverton.

As he entered the town he saw the sheriff's horse outside Anne Denston's, and Dan was soon telling Matt Roberts the results of the watch on the Flying F.

'Shorty would hev finished Goddard off if he'd got on to those steers,' said Roberts, when Dan finished his story. 'Good job he found nothin'.'

Dan nodded. 'What's our next move?' he asked.

'If Stanton's expectin' somethin' to happen tomorrow, we'd better keep tag on them both,' replied Matt thoughtfully. 'You be out at the Flying F before sun-up an' watch Goddard: I'll keep an eye on Stanton an' if the opportunity arises, I'll take a look round the Broken C. Those deeds weren't at Walking A; maybe Stanton has them, an', if so, I'm sure Anne would be mighty interested.'

The first light of a new day was paling the eastern horizon when Dan slipped from his horse and took up his watch on the Flying

F. The ranch was just beginning to come to life when the pound of hoofs thundered hard towards the buildings. Dan stiffened when he saw the dust-covered, hatless foreman of the Flying F hurtling towards the ranch. Dust swirled behind the rider, whose face was covered with blood. Desperately he pulled hard on the reins to bring his horse to a dust-raising halt outside the ranch-house. Walters, who was out of the saddle almost before the horse had stopped, leaped on to the veranda and pounded at the door.

Dan, realising he must know what fresh trouble had hit the Flying F, swung quickly into the saddle, and rode swiftly to the ranch-house into which the cowboy had already been admitted. McCoy hurried to the door and knocked loudly. The door was answered by Goddard's Chinese cook, who, seeing the star on Dan's shirt, quickly showed him to a room across the hall.

As Dan entered the room Goddard swung round to see who his caller was. Dan saw the anger which smouldered in the rancher's eyes.

'Sorry to bother you, Mister Goddard, but Sheriff Roberts wants…' Dan cut his sentence short as he stared past Goddard to

Walters, whose face, caked with blood and dust, was not a pretty sight. Dan looked back at Goddard. 'What's happened?' he asked.

'Fat lot of good you lawmen are!' snarled Goddard viciously. 'Another herd has been rustled, an' you an' Roberts are no nearer findin' out who's doin' it.'

Dan gasped. 'When did this happen?'

'The herd was hit before sun-up,' said Walters. 'Took us completely by surprise. All the night riders were killed. Reckon they took me fer dead. Bullet scraped my head an' knocked me out.' He felt his head gingerly, and winced with the pain. 'I could still hear the herd when I came to, so I followed them. Unfortunately, three of the rustlers had lagged behind pickin' up strays when I stumbled into them. Didn't take me fer one of the herd riders 'cos they told me not to be nosy, beat me up, an' left me unconscious. There was neither sight nor sound of the herd when I came round, but the last I knew of them, they seemed to be headin' fer the hills south-west of the range.'

'A blind,' snapped Goddard. 'There's no grazin' on those hills. They must hev swung in another direction later on. You'd better go an' git yourself fixed up, Dave.'

The foreman pushed himself from the

chair and walked to the door. He paused as he opened it and turned to Goddard.

'I'm sorry, boss,' he apologised dejectedly.

'That's all right,' answered Goddard curtly over his shoulder. As the door closed, Goddard spun on his heel. 'Dave,' he called. When the door opened and the foreman reappeared, the rancher's tone was softer. 'Sorry I snapped, Dave, I know you did your best, but you know how it is; this has hit me hard. I'm afraid this is the end.'

'Don't give up hope, boss,' replied Walters feelingly. 'We'll find those steers.'

As the door closed behind the foreman, Goddard turned to Dan.

'If I hadn't been so weary last night, I'd hev called on McLane an' tackled him about the whole affair. I reckon he's behind it. You lawmen aren't doin' much good, so I figure I'll get over to the Walking A this mornin'.' His lips tightened. 'I'll make thet hombre talk!'

'You're too late, Goddard,' rapped Dan. 'McLane was murdered last night!'

Goddard stared incredulously at Dan. 'What!' he whispered. 'Who did it?'

'Don't know,' replied Dan. 'Matt Roberts an' I were with him. He was about to give us some information when he was shot.'

'Didn't you git the killer?' snapped Goddard.

Dan shook his head. 'He got away from me, near the waterfall at the head of Roaring Valley.'

'We've lost our chance to git a lead on the rustlers,' snapped Goddard, banging his fist into his hand as he paced the room. 'Reckon it's a case of thieves fallin' out.' Suddenly, he slumped into a chair and sighed wearily. 'Wal, I reckon this is really the end fer me,' he said dejectedly.

'But...' started Dan.

'It's no good you lawmen trying to persuade me otherwise,' interrupted the rancher irritatedly. 'What hev you done about it up to now, but ride around in circles?' he snapped.

'I can assure you...' said Dan.

'Assure me nothin',' snarled Goddard. 'It's action an' results thet was needed, but now it's too late; I'm finished!'

The young sheriff felt sorry for the older man and wanted to ease Goddard's mind by telling him all he knew, when he realised that if he did, Goddard, in this frame of mind, would tackle Stanton and give the whole show away, and probably never see his cattle again.

'Finished?' queried Dan. 'Borrow…'

'Borrow?' interrupted Goddard with a derisive laugh. 'I'm already in debt due to tryin' to build up a big herd quickly. After those two herds were rustled, I hed a call from the bank manager wanting to see his money back. He was frightened I wouldn't be able to pay. Thet meant sellin' most of the remainin' cattle, but now, with another seven hundred gone, I'm jest bust.'

'What about your son-in-law?' suggested Dan.

'Tried yesterday, but he couldn't. Wanted to buy this place though,' replied Goddard. 'Maybe thet's what I'll hev to do. Guess I'll ride over there an' see if he'll change his mind about a loan.'

Dan followed Goddard from the house on to the veranda. 'Mind if I go and hev a word with Walters, see if I can pick up a lead?' he asked.

'Do what you like,' replied Goddard, 'but you're wastin' your time.' He swung on his heel, and hurried to the stable.

Dan hung around until the rancher re-appeared with his horse. He strolled casually towards the bunkhouse, watching Goddard carefully, and when he was satisfied that the rancher was settled on his ride, he hurried back to his horse, swung into the saddle, and followed.

Dejectedly, Bill Goddard rode away from the Flying F. All the hard years building up a ranch second to none in this part of Texas had come to nought. It looked as though Stanton would take over, and Goddard felt he would have no say in the running of things under his son-in-law. The rancher shuddered at his thoughts. Suddenly, he straightened himself in the saddle, and a glint came back into his eye as he took a grip on himself.

'Bill Goddard,' he whispered to himself. 'This is no way to be thinkin'. You aren't beaten yet. If Stanton won't change his mind about a loan there are others who...' Doubt crept back into the man's mind, but he shook it off, and sent the horse forward at a faster pace.

Stanton and Pat came on to the veranda to meet him as he halted his horse outside the house. Pat's smile vanished when she saw the worried look on her father's face.

'What's wrong, Dad?' she asked, concern showing in her voice.

'More cattle gone,' replied her father.

'What!' Pat gasped, taking her father by

the arm, and leading him into the house. Stanton followed smiling to himself with the new knowledge that all had gone well the night before, and that Goddard was in a desperate position.

Goddard told them quickly the story of the previous night's happenings. He turned to Stanton when he had finished. 'I'm desperate now, Russ, can't you possibly lend me the money?'

Stanton smiled. 'Wal,' he lied smoothly, 'as a matter of fact I hed somethin' in mind to raise the cash, but now with McLane's death, the Walking A will be coming up fer sale an' I must hev that.' He grinned to himself, wondering what Goddard would say if he knew that he, and not McLane, was the real owner of Roaring Valley.

'But...' Goddard started to protest, but stopped, knowing it was useless.

Pat turned desperately to her husband. 'You can't see...'

Goddard halted her. 'It's no use, Pat, Russ has got his head set, but I must say I thought my son-in-law would hev helped me. However, don't worry, Pat, I've a few friends in town whom I think will raise the cash fer me.' Goddard turned and strode from the house.

Pat swung sharply on her husband, tears welling in her eyes. 'You can't let him go, you must help him.' She flung herself pleadingly at Stanton, who laughed loudly, and pushed her roughly out of the way. Pat fell sobbing into a chair as Stanton strode slowly from the house.

He reached the veranda to find Jed Roscoe sitting on the rail examining his rifle. Stanton leaned on the rail beside him, and the two men watched Goddard ride away, without speaking.

'You know, Jed,' said Stanton, breaking the silence. 'I think it would be better if Mister Goddard did not reach his friends in town.'

Jed grinned. 'Jest as you say, boss. This old rifle will notch up a third.'

The squeak of the door behind them made Stanton spin round. He leaped forward and flung the door open, to find Pat standing close to it. She tried to move quickly past him, opening her mouth to yell a warning to her father, but the sound was stifled in her throat as Stanton's hand pressed hard over her lips, and his other arm encircled her waist tightly.

'No you don't,' he snarled. 'Those words were not meant for pretty little ears like yours.' He turned, nodded to Roscoe, who grinned evilly, and hurried to the stable.

Pat, her eyes wide with terror, struggled desperately, but Stanton's grip was too tight. She saw Roscoe lead the horse from the stable, swing into the saddle, and ride to the house.

'I'm sorry, Mrs Stanton,' he mocked, 'but this is the best way for my boss to get the Flying F. You will soon inherit it.'

Stanton laughed, and released his grip. 'It's no use yelling now, your father's too far away.' He shoved her roughly against the wall, and turned to his foreman. 'Not too near the ranch, Jed.'

'Stop! Stop! It's no use,' cried Pat, 'the ranch won't be mine!'

Stanton turned on her in amazement. 'What! You're lying!'

Pat shook her head, hoping desperately that Stanton would believe her. 'It won't!' she shouted. 'Dad made a new will the day before we were married.'

Stanton glanced at her, hardly able to believe his ears. He grabbed her by the shoulders; his eyes, flaming with rage, stared deeply into hers. 'You're lying! You're lying!' he yelled.

'I'm not!' cried Pat frantically. 'I didn't want the Flying F when I was coming here.

I persuaded Dad to leave it to Dave Walters; he's been with Dad since the start.'

'You fool!' shouted Stanton. Hate smouldered in his eyes. He pushed himself away from his sobbing wife. 'Roscoe,' he snapped at his foreman. 'Git after Goddard; tell him thet Pat an' I hev got some information about his cattle; bring him to the valley.'

Roscoe nodded, and kicked his horse into a gallop after Goddard.

Stanton turned to Pat, and grabbed her wrists. She stared wide-eyed at her husband. 'I was suspicious of you,' she whispered, 'but you're in this deeper than I thought you were.' Pat gasped. 'McLane! How did you know McLane was dead? Nobody had been here to tell us, and yet you mentioned buying the Walking A! It was you that...' The sentence died on her lips as the full realisation of the truth struck her.

Stanton laughed harshly in her face. 'Roscoe's handy with a rifle when I want him to be. I put McLane in the Walking A after Roscoe had got rid of John Denston fer me. McLane was a blind for your father who I figured would fight fer Roaring Valley if I took it over. All I wanted then, was the Flying F, thet's why I married you, an' after I'd got the ranch, it wouldn't hev been long before Shirley Parker was my wife. It won't be long now, either,' smirked Stanton, dragging Pat forward towards the stables. 'After your father has been persuaded to change his will, you and he will disappear.'

Pat struggled desperately, but her husband forced her towards the stables and into the saddle. They left the Broken C at a fast gallop, unaware that two lawmen watched them go.

Dan kept a convenient distance behind Bill Goddard on his ride to the Broken C, and halted by the cover of some trees from which he watched the rancher ride up to the house, to be greeted by the Stantons. Dan saw them go inside, and as he swung from the saddle, he heard a low whistle to his left. Looking round, he saw Matt Roberts waving to him from the cover of some bushes. He tied his horse to a tree, and crept swiftly to join the Sheriff of Silverton.

'Glad to see you, Dan,' greeted Matt, keeping the tone of his voice low. 'Nothin's happened around here, yet.'

Dan told him quickly about the latest rustling of Flying F cattle, and of his interview with Goddard.

'Guess we jest settle down an' await

developments,' said Roberts when Dan had finished his story.

The two men watched the house and neighbouring buildings carefully. Dan started when he saw Jed Roscoe emerge from the bunkhouse, and glanced in the direction of the main building.

'Roscoe!' gasped Dan. 'It can't have been him I chased up the valley.' He glanced at Roberts. 'Then who could hev killed Mc-Lane?'

'Don't be too sure, Dan,' said Matt. 'Roscoe's smart; he might hev tricked you. I've learned that there's a hollow behind thet waterfall. Roscoe could hev hidden behind it.'

'But,' replied Dan, annoyed by the mystery, 'I saw his sombrero.'

'Thet could hev been thrown into the water,' said Matt. 'If he...'

His words were cut short when Dan indicated to him to keep silent and nodded towards the ranch. Roscoe, who had gone back into the bunkhouse had reappeared with a rifle and strolled casually to the ranch-house to sit on the rail near the door.

'Trouble?' queried Matt.

Dan shrugged his shoulders, and eased the Colt in its holster.

The minutes went by, but suddenly the lawmen tensed themselves when they saw Goddard hurry from the house and without so much as a glance at Roscoe, swing into the saddle, and ride away at a fast trot.

'You'd better follow him,' said Matt, as he watched Goddard.

'Wait a minute,' whispered Dan, gripping the sheriff's arm, and nodding towards the ranch-house.

Stanton had come on to the veranda, and was talking to his foreman and nodding in the direction taken by Goddard.

Suddenly, Dan gasped, his hand flew to his Colt when he saw Stanton turn sharply and grab Pat. Dan would have leaped into the open, but Matt restrained him.

'Hold on,' advised Matt. 'Let's see what happens.'

The two men fixed their attention on the scene before them, and it took all of Dan's self-control to stop himself from going to help Pat as he saw her roughly treated by her husband. The two men watched the scene unfold, and when Roscoe rode off in the same direction as Goddard Matt turned to Dan.

'Better git after Roscoe,' he said. 'Seems as though he has to tail Goddard.' Matt saw

Dan hesitate and glance in the direction of the house where Stanton forcibly held Pat. 'Go on,' urged the sheriff, 'I'll keep an eye on things here. No harm will come to Pat.'

Dan nodded, and crept quickly to his horse and set off on Roscoe's trail.

Sheriff Matt Roberts hated watching the rough treatment of Pat, but he knew if he intervened it would ruin the chances of finding Goddard's stolen cattle. When Stanton dragged Pat to the stables and reappeared with two horses, Matt realised he was in a dilemma. He wanted to trail Stanton, but he knew that with no other cowhands around, this was his chance to search the house for the deeds of the Walking A.

He watched the two riders turn from the ranch, and after noting the direction they took, he climbed on to his horse and rode swiftly to the ranch-house. Realising his horse would be less conspicuous at the back of the house, he took it to the rear of the building, tied the animal to the rail, and hurried to the door. He pushed it open and stepped quickly inside, where the Chinese cook looked surprised to find himself staring into the cold muzzle of a Colt.

'No sound,' snapped Matt. 'Anyone else

around the house?'

The cook, his eyes wide with terror, shook his head.

'Turn round,' ordered the sheriff.

The Chinaman stared to shake. 'Please, no shoot,' he pleaded.

Impatiently, Matt motioned with his Colt and reluctantly the cook shuffled round. The sheriff stepped forward quickly, raised his gun, and with one sharp swift movement whipped the barrel across the Chinaman's head. The cook's knees buckled, and without a sound he pitched to the floor.

Matt hurried through the house until he saw Stanton's large desk which stood across the corner of one room. The sheriff, knowing that with every minute his task of catching up with, and trailing Stanton, was being made more difficult, searched the drawers quickly but found no documents relating to the Walking A. Almost in despair, he grabbed the knob of the last drawer, but found it was locked. He snatched the paper-knife, which lay on the desk and inserted it at the top of the drawer. After a few moments prising, the wood splintered, and the lock gave way. Eagerly he pulled the drawer open to find a number of neatly folded documents which he looked through quickly. As he turned over the last document, dismay filled the sheriff. He was still as far off finding the deeds to the Walking A as he was when he started.

He glanced round the room quickly, wondering where he should search next. A corner cupboard attracted his attention, and Matt jumped to his feet, putting the documents back into the drawer as he did so. His hand caught the bottom of the drawer and the slight tap made him look down, thinking there was something unusual about it. He tapped the wood harder getting a hollow sound. Matt pulled the drawer completely out of the desk and examining it quickly noticed that the depth inside was about two inches less than that outside.

'A false bottom!' whispered Matt jerking his Colt from its holster. Turning the gun round, he held it by the barrel and with one blow shattered the bottom of the drawer. He shoved the Colt back into the leather and excitedly tore the wood away from the drawer to find several documents. Eagerly he looked them over and a shout of triumph escaped from his lips when he saw the deeds for which he had been searching.

He pushed himself to his feet, pocketed the documents, and stepped from behind the desk as the door opened, and Shorty Best walked into the room. The gunman stopped in his tracks, his eyes widening with surprise when he saw the sheriff. He glanced at the shattered remains of the drawer on the desk. In a flash his hand flew for his gun but Matt, who had momentarily been taken aback by the appearance of Shorty, was faster. His Colt roared and the cowboy staggered back against the doorpost as the bullet thudded into him. His hand tugged his gun from its holster but Matt squeezed the trigger again and the lead jerked Shorty against the wall. It supported him momentarily before his knees buckled and he slid slowly to the floor. His finger tightened on the trigger, but the bullet buried itself harmlessly in the floorboards. As the cowboy shuddered and lay still, Matt shoved his smoking Colt back into its holster and striding over the body, hurried outside to his horse.

The sheriff leaped into the saddle and kicked his horse into a gallop away from the Broken C, hoping that Stanton was still heading in the same direction.

## Chapter Sixteen

Sheriff Matt Roberts urged his horse faster across the range and earth flew under the pounding hoofs as the animal stretched itself in answer to its rider's call. The lawman was anxious to catch sight of the two riders before they reached the rough country which lay across their path.

As the ground flew beneath him, Matt continually searched the landscape ahead for a glimpse of his quarry. Suddenly, a smile split his face and the tension in his body relaxed. He eased himself in the saddle and slowed the horse's headlong gallop, although he kept to a good pace in order to close the gap before Stanton and Pat reached the rough country. Once in the hills their speed slackened and although the trail twisted and turned, the lawman had little difficulty in following the track of the two riders.

Stanton kept to a steady pace and around the head of Roaring Valley, across the Flying F range and soon Matt realised that they were heading for the hills in the extreme south-west of Goddard's land.

'Must be wastin' my time,' he muttered to himself. 'The cattle can't be there, grazin's too poor.' In spite of his doubts the sheriff stuck grimly to his task of trailing Stanton.

The pace slackened once again as the land rose towards the higher ground and when the trail steepened in the hills Matt pulled his horse to a halt behind some boulders. He was close to the riders and, as they twisted up the side of the hill, he knew he would risk discovery if he followed too closely. The sheriff slipped from the saddle, crouched beside the rocks, and watched the progress of the rancher and his wife. Suddenly, Stanton turned to his left and almost before Matt realised it, the two riders had disappeared round the side of the hill.

He jumped to his feet and swung quickly into the saddle. Showers of small stones were sent tumbling down the hillside as Matt urged his horse over the rough ground. The sheriff was trying to estimate the place at which Stanton had turned when suddenly there was a break in the rise of the hill and he found himself on a flat stretch of ground about fifty yards wide which ran round the side of the hill.

A shout of triumph came to Matt's lips when he saw this track had been beaten by hundreds of hoofs.

Eagerly, he pulled his horse round sending it in the direction taken by Stanton. As the track swung round the side of the hill, narrowed and started to climb, Matt realised that expert cowboys had handled the cattle along such a track. A hill rose steeply on the left and the ground steepened towards a ridge ahead. Nearing the ridge Matt halted, scouted the land ahead, and seeing no sign of movement, he moved cautiously forward. Suddenly, the sheriff jerked hard on the reins surprised at the sight which confronted him. A small valley bounded by steep cliffs lay below him and hundreds of steers grazed intently on the lush grass. A tree-lined stream flowed through the valley, and a hut occupied a central position close to the water. Immediately in front of him the ridge fell away to the floor of the valley. A track wound down the side of the hill and Matt, realising there was no other way into the valley, could not help admiring the men who had handled cattle over such country.

'Goddard's cattle!' Matt whispered to himself. 'No wonder we couldn't find them!'

Stanton and Pat were almost at the bottom of the hill and Matt waited patiently, watching them, until they reached the hut. He noted that only one man came to meet them, and guessed the rest of the rustlers must be further along the valley where he could see signs of activity near a fire.

Roberts slipped from the saddle and led the horse along the ridge to the shelter of some rocks. He checked his Colt and using every precaution to keep his presence a secret, made his way slowly down the hillside towards the nearest trees. Keeping close to the water's edge, and using the cover afforded by the trees and bushes, Matt crept carefully towards the hut. A few yards from the building the sheriff halted and took stock of his surroundings. There was no sign of anyone returning from along the valley, and the sound of voices talking earnestly drifted through the open window close to the door.

Matt eased his Colt from its holster, stepped from his cover and ran swiftly and silently to the hut where he flattened himself against the wall and inched his way along until he crouched beneath the window.

'Wal, Butch,' drawled Stanton. 'It won't be long before we can tie this thing up. The

Flying F will soon be mine, an' in a week or so I'll discover the rustled cattle.'

'But the rustlers escape,' added Butch, with a chuckle. 'We're already altering some of the brands.'

'Good work,' complimented Stanton. 'Cattle king of Silverton,' he went on, his voice toned with pride and greed. 'An' I'll run thet town to suit myself.'

Matt moved quickly to the door, and with a sharp kick knocked it open.

'Hold it!' he rapped, as the two men surprised and startled by the sudden intrusion reached for their Colts. The menace of Matt's gun froze the rustlers' grip to the butts of their weapons. Slowly they released their hold, and let their hands drop by their sides.

A cry of relieved surprise came from Pat when she saw the sheriff. The girl moved quickly to the door and closed it.

'Get the guns, Pat,' said the sheriff tersely, and Pat, who moved behind the two men, relieved them of their weapons. 'With a shade of luck we should git these hombres to Silverton by dark.'

Pat looked startled. 'We can't go yet!' she announced, alarm showing in her voice.

'Why not?' rapped Matt curtly.

'Russ sent Roscoe to bring my father here,' explained Pat. 'They should be here soon.' She looked pleadingly at the sheriff. 'We can't leave my father at the mercy of Roscoe.'

Matt frowned, but answered the girl reassuringly. 'All right, Pat, we'll jest hev to wait.'

'Thet's right,' laughed Stanton. 'Smart girl to think of thet. Every minute you're held up here lessens your chances of escape. Better give…'

'Shut up!' snapped the sheriff. 'Pat keep watch out of thet window; we don't want any of those men from along the valley surprisin' us.'

Pat crossed to the window which afforded her a good view, but there was no sign of any of the branding party returning, and the smoke from their fire still curled lazily on the still air.

Matt indicated two chairs. 'Sit down,' he ordered.

Stanton turned to Butch. 'Guess we may as well take the weight off our feet, although it won't be for long. When do you think they'll finish brandin'?'

Butch grinned. 'I told the boys to do only a few fer you to see before we tackled the main bunch. Reckon they shouldn't be long now.'

Matt stared coldly at the two men without speaking. He wanted to look out of the window and watch for Roscoe, but he knew that if he gave Stanton and Butch half a chance, they would be upon him the moment he relaxed his vigilance. Realising his only chance with Roscoe was to surprise him when he entered the hut he moved to one side of the door so that when the door opened he would be hidden from view.

'What's the matter, sheriff?' laughed Stanton when he saw the lawman move. 'Gettin' jittery?'

'Keep quiet,' snapped Matt, 'an' act natural when Roscoe comes in here.'

Time seemed to hang still to Matt Roberts and Pat as they waited. Stanton moved his hand to his pocket.

'Hold it!' snapped Matt, 'keep your hand out of there!'

Stanton looked at the sheriff in amazement. There was a touch of mockery in his voice when he spoke. 'What's this? Sheriff Matt Roberts gettin' jumpy. I was only reachin' fer a cheroot.' A grin spread across his face. 'May I git one, sheriff?'

Matt eyed him suspiciously, then nodded.

Stanton drew two cheroots from his pocket and handed one to Butch. 'I won't offer you one, Matt, it would take your attention away from us whilst you lit it an' thet would never do,' he said sarcastically.

The two men lit their cheroots. Stanton drew deeply and blew a long smoke cloud into the air before he spoke again.

'Better give up, Matt; when the boys finish brandin' you'll never hold out alone. If you want...'

The words were halted as the door began to open slowly. Stanton moved slowly to his feet, staring at the doorway. He glanced sharply at Matt who tensed himself behind the door waiting for the two men to come in. For a moment nothing happened; the sheriff was puzzled by the fact that there was no movement. He looked at Stanton and Butch trying to read in their faces what was happening behind the door. He glanced at Pat who was turning slowly from the window, but before she could show any emotion, Roscoe spoke.

'All right, sheriff, jest drop thet gun,' he rapped. 'Goddard's stood right in front of me an' could catch the full blast, but right at this moment I'm aimin' at Mrs Stanton.'

A grin spread across Stanton's face. 'Don't

be afraid to let her have it Jed if the sheriff doesn't do as he's told, but save Goddard until after he's altered his will.'

Roberts hesitated. The grin disappeared from Stanton's face, his eyes narrowed. 'Wal, Roberts,' he snapped viciously. 'We're waitin'.'

Matt, realising he was in a hopeless position, threw down his gun. Stanton and Butch recovered their Colts, and Roscoe shoved Goddard forward roughly into the hut where Pat flung herself sobbing into her father's arms.

'Well done, Jed,' congratulated Stanton. 'How did you know he was here?'

'We were climbing towards the ridge an' saw him jest before he started into the valley,' explained Roscoe. 'Watched him ever since.'

'Good work.' Stanton turned to Goddard. 'We'll get down to business, Goddard,' he grinned. 'I tried to force you to sell the Flying F but you wouldn't, so I'm jest goin' to hev to put my other plans into operation.'

'You are behind everything!' gasped Goddard. 'Until Roscoe spoke jest now, I thought you'd found my cattle, an'...'

'I found your cattle all right,' laughed Stanton. I told Roscoe to bring you to see them an' I thought you might like to alter your will at the same time.'

'Will?' Goddard stared incredulously at Stanton.

'Yeah,' replied Stanton. 'You alter your will so that Pat gits the Flying F when you die – an' you'll die soon,' he added with a grin. 'After thet it won't be long before I'm a widower and the Flying F will be mine!'

Startled by Stanton's implications, Goddard stiffened. He looked at Pat. 'What's this all about, Pat? I don't understand; what's happened to Russ? This isn't the man you married.'

Pat, tears in her eyes looked lovingly at her father. 'Oh yes, it is, Dad. He doesn't appear the same to you, but I suspected he was up to something when I overheard Roscoe an' Best talking one night near the Flying F. Dad, I didn't want any harm to come to you so I married Russ to find out what his game was. I knew he wanted to marry me, and I hoped that if I did, it would stop whatever he was planning to do to you. I was wrong, he only wanted me as a means of getting the Flying F if his rustling failed to force your hand.'

Hate filled Goddard's eyes as he stared at Stanton. 'To think I persuaded Pat to marry

211

you instead of Lance Peters. I wanted to see us running a cattle empire, but you were running far ahead of me.'

Stanton grinned. 'Yeah, far ahead. Pat hasn't quite finished the story, you may as well know the rest.' He calmly re-lit his cheroot, watching Goddard all the time. 'Thet cattle empire you talk about has been my ambition fer some time, but with only me running it. First I hed to hev Roaring Valley, so John Denston was put out of the way at a time which I knew was inconvenient fer you to buy it. I put McLane in there as a cover. McLane was gettin' out of hand, so he was treated the same as Denston, an' when you hev altered your will you'll go the same way.'

Goddard and Roberts half moved towards Stanton but the cold muzzle of a Colt halted them. Goddard looked at his daughter. 'What's all this about my will?'

'Russ sent Roscoe to kill you when you left the Broken C,' explained Pat. 'I told him it was no good killing you because you had changed your will and the ranch wouldn't be mine.'

The sudden realisation that he had been tricked struck Stanton hard. 'So your father didn't alter the will,' he snapped.

'No.' There was a tone of contempt and mockery in Pat's voice.

Stanton jumped forward. 'You little brat,' he snarled, and brought his hand viciously across her face, sending her reeling across the room, to crash against the wall.

In spite of the guns Goddard leaped at Stanton, crashing his fist into his face. Matt made to move forward, but Butch's gun menaced him, and he had to watch Roscoe grab Goddard and hurl him against the table.

Dark anger and hate flared across Stanton's face. He raised his gun, and levelled it at the Flying F rancher. Pat lay sobbing against the wall.

'Don't!' she cried desperately.

Stanton lowered his gun slowly, an evil smile slowly crossing his face. 'You come near to it then,' he whispered between tightened lips. 'But first you can watch your daughter die, it matters little who dies first now.'

He turned his gun towards the crumpled form of the wide-eyed terror-stricken Pat.

Suddenly the hut was filled with a deafening roar of a Colt and everyone stared incredulously for a moment at the folding form of Russ Stanton as he sank to the floor. Seizing the opportunity of diverted attentions, Matt Roberts leaped forward, crashing his fist against Butch's chin as another shot rang out. He jumped after the cowboy bringing his knee into the rustler's stomach as he crashed into the wall. With a gasp the wind was driven from his body and Matt grasped his wrist twisting the Colt from his grasp. The sheriff stepped back to see Roscoe nursing a painful shattered wrist and Dan McCoy entering the hut.

'Good work, Dan,' said Matt with a grin. 'I'm mighty glad to see you.'

Goddard was by his daughter's side, helping her to her feet. 'It's all right, Pat, it's all right,' he comforted. He turned to face the two lawmen. 'I don't understand how you two...' His words were cut short by the pound of hoofs some distance along the valley.

'The shots must hev been heard by the branding party,' gasped Matt. 'Here Pat, watch Roscoe an' Butch.' He handed the girl a Colt who motioned the two men to one corner of the hut and kept the gun levelled at them.

Dan was already at the window. 'Seven,' he said as Matt Roberts and Bill Goddard joined him.

'Yeah,' drawled Matt. 'Thet's Charlie from the Walking A in front – so thet's how they knew their way around at night so easily. The other six will be Butch's gang.'

'Only two of us can use this window,' said Dan. 'I'm goin' to make a dash for the trees near the water; I reckon I might be more use outside.'

'Don't chance it,' said Matt, trying to restrain the young man.

'I'll hev surprise on my side,' pointed out Dan. 'I'll be half way to cover before they realise it, an' when you see them go fer their guns, let them have it.' The sheriff from Red Springs crossed to the door and waited until Matt gave him the signal.

As soon as Roberts raised his hand Dan flung open the door and with a crouching run, was over half way to cover before the rustlers knew what was happening.

At the same time, Roberts and Goddard sent a volley of shots from the hut. The riders pulled hard on the reins, bringing their horses to an earth-tearing, sliding halt, and almost in the same movement twisting the animals round away from the lead. Charlie grabbed for his gun, but before he could draw it a bullet drove into his chest toppling him from his horse. Animals

215

screamed as bullets nicked them, and they crashed one against the other. The men leaped from their saddles, diving for cover but one did not make it as a shot hit the back of his neck. Two of the rustlers loosed off shots at Dan who, as the bullets sprayed the ground at his feet, dived for the protecting shelter of the trees. He hit the ground hard and rolled over, panting for breath. Dan fired two shots in the direction of the rustlers and then crept quickly to more advantageous cover.

As the rustlers gained cover Matt and Goddard eased their fire and picked their targets with more care. The sheriff, spotting a movement amongst some bushes, took careful aim and knew he had found his target when a man pitched forward to lay still.

'Thet leaves four,' muttered Matt.

Goddard nodded and almost at the same moment reeled back as lead whined through the window digging deep into his shoulder. As her father staggered Pat cried out with alarm and half turned to him. Butch, seizing the opportunity leaped forward grasping the girl's wrist and tried to pull her round in front of him. Suddenly a great roar filled the hut; Butch's grasp slackened and Pat staggered away from him horrified as she saw him crumple to the floor at her feet. She stared stupidly at the smoking Colt in her hand, hardly able to believe what had happened. Matt who had gone to help Goddard, menaced Roscoe with his Colt and moved quickly to Pat's side.

'You all right?' he asked anxiously.

Words choked in the girl's throat; she nodded unable to speak.

Goddard moved across to his daughter. 'It's only my shoulder, Pat. Give me the gun, I'll watch Roscoe. Matt you'd better git back to thet window.'

Dan was startled when the firing from the hut ceased. He glanced anxiously towards the building but received no indication of what was happening inside. Suddenly a shot rang out and it took Dan all his self control to stop from dashing to the hut, but he realised he would never make it. The rustlers had ceased firing and thinking they might attempt to rush the hut he sent two shots in their direction, reminding them that he still had them covered. Relief swept over Dan when a Colt crashed from the hut and as the firing continued Dan decided to try to circle the rustlers.

He slipped quickly to the water's edge and

was soon at the other side of the stream. Crouching, he hurried swiftly from cover to cover until he had moved beyond the group of men who faced the hut. He re-crossed the stream and crept slowly towards the rustlers. The four men were close together and were giving the hut their full attention. 'What's happened to thet other hombre?' said one of the rustlers.

'Maybe we hit him,' came the reply.

'Better make sure, go an' hev a look, an' then circle the hut and see if we can git at it from the other side,' ordered the first man.

The second cowboy nodded and turned to go when Dan's voice rapped out, 'Stay where you are an' drop your guns.'

Startled, the men spun around, one jerking his Colt upwards, but Dan squeezed his trigger before the man could fire, and the rustler crashed backwards to the ground and lay still. Under the menace of Dan's smoking gun the remaining three rustlers dropped their guns.

'Right,' snapped Dan, 'turn around, put your hands up, and start walking.'

Matt stared at the bushes wondering why the firing had ceased.

'What's happening?' asked Goddard.

'Don't know,' replied Matt. 'Maybe they're

cookin' up somethin' fer us.'

A shot shattered the silence but Matt was puzzled when no bullet hit the hut. Suddenly he yelled with surprise. 'Dan's got them! He's bringin' them in!'

Matt and Pat ran to the door to meet Dan as he marched the rustlers to the hut.

'Good work, Dan,' complimented Matt.

'I was worried when I heard the shot inside the hut,' said Dan. 'What happened?'

Matt quickly explained and soon all the prisoners were tied ready for the ride back to Silverton.

'Think you can make it?' Dan asked Goddard.

'Yeah, sure I can,' replied the rancher with a grin. 'I'm mighty grateful to you two, but I still haven't figured how you found us.'

'We've been suspicious of Stanton for some time,' explained Roberts, 'but we hed no proof. Dan overheard Stanton tell Shorty Best that he'd be expectin' you after thet last rustlin' an' thet things would start to move, so we took the precaution of trailin' you both. Dan followed Roscoe when he set off after you an' I kept my eye on Stanton, who left the Broken C with Pat. Nearly lost them when I stayed behind to search the house.'

'Search? What for?' puzzled Pat.

'The deeds to the Walking A,' explained Matt.

'Thet job was planned by Stanton so thet he could get the deeds when Anne was out of the house looking for her husband,' said Dan. He turned to Matt. 'Did you find them?'

'Sure,' grinned Matt, pulling the deeds from his pocket. 'Anne is sure goin' to get a surprise when I tell her she can go back to the Walking A.'

Dan turned to Goddard. 'Reckon you'll hev new neighbours there,' he said. 'Mr and Mrs Matt Roberts!'

'Nothin' I'd like better,' laughed Goddard.

'What are you goin' to do with the Broken C?' asked Matt. 'It will be yours now, Pat.'

'I don't know,' replied Pat, shaking her head.

'I do,' Goddard roared. 'She's goin' to become Mrs Lance Peters and work the spread. I'm sorry I was pushing about Stanton.'

Pat smiled and kissed her father.

'Never could understand why Pat married Stanton after thet first day I saw her,' said Dan.

Pat explained her reason as Dan led her from the hut. 'You'd better stay fer the double wedding,' Pat invited as she finished her story.

Matt approved, but Dan shook his head.

'Thanks a lot,' he said, 'but I've got to get back to Red Springs. Guess I'll never get there if I keep gettin' curious on the trail.'

The publishers hope that this book has given you enjoyable reading. Large Print Books are especially designed to be as easy to see and hold as possible. If you wish a complete list of our books please ask at your local library or write directly to:

**Dales Large Print Books**
Magna House, Long Preston,
Skipton, North Yorkshire.
BD23  4ND